Sanjay Sharma represented India in badminton from 1975 to 1990. He was appointed as the captain of the Indian team for the 1989 Asian championship and 1990 Commonwealth games and later served as the national coach from 1988 to 2003. He has won a record 19 Maharashtra state championship titles.

During his badminton days, Sanjay won some very crucial matches for India. Apart from being a shuttler, he also became an ace journalist and TV commentator, fought a pitched battle with the BAI and came out trumps.

Also by Sanjay Sharma

Match Point: A Shuttler's Story

Courage Beyond Compare: How Ten Athletes Overcame
Disability and Adversity to Emerge Champions

Pullela Gopi Chand: The World Beneath His Feat

PRAISE FOR THE BOOK

**Dr Ameeta Sinh, Ex International Badminton Player,
Ex Minister, Govt of Uttar Pradesh**

'Descriptive, immersive and imaginative! Captivating the reader and taking them on a sensory tour of the events that take place. Feels like a reel running before your eyes. This book is a must read! A thoroughly enjoyable read this book is; a sure shot it hit!'

Ramveer Tanwar, PondMan, Environmentalist, Founder of Say Earth, TEDx Speaker

'How responsible is the state when it comes to perpetuating rape culture? The question the book seeks to address is who to raise the first voice against, while arguing that the state of India has played 'an active and collusive role' in violating human and civil rights especially when it comes to sexual violence. Sanjay Sharma has looked at sexual violence in rural parts of our country that is often ignored and left unjustified. It is important to break the silence surrounding rape culture as well as the need for resistance. This book is critical in understanding state impunity when it comes to rape culture.'

Ashutosh Tiwari, General Secretary at Better World Foundation and Astrologer at Astrotalk

'We all hear stories of women molestation; you may have heard stories of revenge of some women; but this book will show you an in-depth, personal psyche of a serial rapist, what made him a rapist, and when he meets his nemesis, we also see that her metal is created by hardships. A thrilling but truthful account of what happens when a lecherous criminal who has raped more than 200 women is hackled in broad daylight. A psychological thriller with real life inspiration.'

Manju Pathak, President of Mahila Adhikar Sangthan, Prayagraj

'The way the author described the troubles and torments of a woman is perfectly splendid. This novel tells us that a woman must stand for her rights on her own and fight with the darkness consuming her, regardless of whom she is backed by. And if a woman fights for herself against a society full of rotten mentally, she doesn't only bring justice for herself, but she also stops the crime inflicted on other women, too. I send warm regards and gratitude to the author from the entire women's society. Thank you.'

Nandini Mishra, General Secretary at Mahila Prabodhini Foundation

Sexual harassment and rape are a reality that stalks most women and girls. Yet, the cry of our daughters, sisters, and mothers remains unheard; they remain within the walls of their homes, silenced by the administration, fear of what society might say, a false sense of family pride or social pressure, and so on. In between all this chaos and dilemma, the victim fails to raise their voice. The author, Sanjay Sharma has remarkably pen-locked the story stating the mentality that births a rapist. It is not like anyone is born a rapist, but the circumstances make them destructive.

MUKTI
THE SALVATION

SANJAY SHARMA

Inkfeathers Publishing
www.inkfeathers.com

Published by Inkfeathers Pvt. Ltd
84, Janta Flats, Vivek Vihar
New Delhi 110095, Delhi, India

Mukti—The Salvation
Written by Sanjay Sharma
Paperback Edition

First Published by Inkfeathers Publishing India 2022
Edited by Arjun Yadav & Uma Bokil

ISBN 9789390882489

www.inkfeathers.com

This book is dedicated to all women who have suffered but have come back strongly to defend themselves against their tormentors, especially with no help coming from general society, the police, or law courts.

I also dedicate this book to the three women in my life; my wife, Deepti and my two daughters, Medini and Shachi, who were the pillars of my life in every way.
Without them, I would not have survived my major illness and surgeries and hospitalisation. I can't thank them enough for all they have done for me.

DISCLAIMER

Bearing resemblance to the Nagpur rape case of 2003, which is in public domain, only and only the character of the rapist and action-taking women are inspired by the real life scenario. This work does not aim to document the real-life incidents or the real happenings in any manner whatsoever. All the other elements of the story, names, characters, objects, businesses, places, events, incidents, whether physical/non-physical, real/unreal, tangible/intangible in whatsoever description used in this book are either the product of the author's imagination or used in a fictitious manner. Any other resemblance than mentioned above to actual persons, objects, entities, living or dead, is purely coincidental. This book is recommended for ages 16 and older due to intense use of abuse of language and vivid descriptions of sex, rape, and slang. The work does not, in any way, encourage citizens to deviate from the law.

FOREWORD

Sanjay Sharma correctly asks a question. Why should women suffer silently? When they try to raise a voice, the police shuns them, and local politicians take advantage of them. But if continuously hounded by antisocial elements, rapists or extortionists, is it a sin bigger than rape, if, to save themselves, they take law into their own hands? The hounded women in Mukti, raped and raped again by Bhiku, finally found their voice and decided to kill him at first opportunity. Were they right?

The author correctly justified this action by the women. They got rid of an evil man who mercilessly battered them to brink of their dignity. Sanjay has woven a very intricate tale which hits you in your guts. Every character portrayed has been put a lot of thought into and has a definite place in the story. Though Bhiku is very anti-women, the two women in his life have their own reasons to be what they are. One cannot blame them for turning against him. The juvenile correctional facility and the central jail where he is sent makes him a die-hard criminal. The jail sequences are electrifying.

How Bhiku is killed in a well-planned move is the essence of Mukti. The story brings out how the victims attain salvation; mukti, that is, freedom. It is a wonderful story; you would not like to leave any page unturned; a gripping tale which makes you start from the first page all over again.

After a very long time a scintillating and outstanding book has come.

I urge you not to miss it.

—Nilamber Kaushik, award-winning, renowned Hindi author (Aakhri Daon, Sajish, Badla)

CONTENTS

THE ANTICIPATION

It was a typical late afternoon in a small town located near Jabalpur called Chandanpur, known for its sizzling heat during summer. The heat wave was at its peak and orange orchards conducted their brisk business while the tamarind trees were heavy and laden with ripe fruits. The mangoes, on the other hand, were fully ripe and nearing their harvest time. If one stepped outside on roads before 4 p.m., they could actually observe fumes surging out from the road surfaces as the tar on them blazed in the extreme heat. In Chandanpur, colleges and coaching classes were scheduled from early morning 8 a.m. to 1 p.m. so that kids could relax and have their siestas.

But as rest of the town actually slept, or rested over from the extreme heat, Rinkunagar (a settlement located near the station where residents lived cheek-by-jowl) was inebriated with a buzz about Bhiku Karandikar finally meeting his nemesis at the city criminal court, where he was to appear as a defendant against multiple rape and murder charges. His case was posted for 4:30 p.m. in the court of Justice

Inamdar.

The women of Rinkunagar had not slept the whole night as they all pondered over the fact that Bhiku had appeared in numerous cases brought in by the residents of this slum, but somehow had escaped justice. The reasoning behind it was clear; at the local police *thana* where Senior Inspector Kamble ruled the roost, the FIRs filed were totally insipid and filled with enough loopholes, allowing him to escape the clutches of justice every time. All such cases were dropped against him each time they were brought up.

Most residents of Rinkunagar were illiterate, and even if they could read or write a bit, the legal jargon that went in filing an FIR was way beyond their intellectual capabilities. Furthermore, there existed the humiliating experience of having to undergo a medical check-up to ensure that the integrity of the women had been savaged, to ensure if yes— rape had actually taken place. During the check-ups, the constables would grin lecherously, making the victim squirm with indignity. In fact, a couple of times, the policeman would molest the poor victim who was brave enough to file an FIR.

As the afternoon wore on and the sun started shedding its heat, the buzz became louder and deeper within the slum. The one question uppermost in the minds of these countless victims was simple—will Bhiku escape again and come back to torment them? Not only did he pay a decent *hafta* or weekly bribe to Kamble and his cohorts, but it was also an accepted fact that he had blackmailed some of these helpless, hapless, and poor women to accompany Kamble at some isolated areas outside the city to satisfy his lust.

Even the Local MLA Rana Patil had a hand in ensuring that Bhiku was never convicted, never jailed. Patil was a huge beneficiary in Bhiku's scheme of things. So, with the police and local *'Bahubali'* politician in his pocket, Bhiku had an uninterrupted run of the place. No one dared to oppose him.

He had stopped counting, but the hassled slum dwellers said he had raped, sodomised, and brutalised more than 200 females from Rinkunagar. It was presumed that there existed a victim of his savagery from every second shanty located in Rinkunagar. Even more disgusting was the fact that his victims ranged from 60 years of age to a 12-year-old girl. He himself was 32 years old, unemployed, and living off extorting money from the traumatised victims. He had a track record of murdering 30-odd people; thus, who would dare to question him or his motives? He would rape young mothers in front of their families and young girls in front of their parents. In short, Bhiku was the manifestation of pure evil.

Today, too, he was confident of his release and was already informing Sr. Inspector Kamble of their feast over drinks and dinner. "After dinner, you suggest a place and I will bring 3-4 young ones. We will celebrate whole night," he whispered to Kamble, winking to convey the message. With a cheesy smile on his disgraceful face, Kamble winked back.

****

Bhiku was being escorted by Kamble to the sessions court. As he finished the formalities and documentation, Bhiku reminded him about enjoying at night after he got bailed.

They were outside the main gate of the Central Jail, waiting to get in the police van, and did not notice a group of few women who were standing next to an autorickshaw that was parked.

Bhiku was very sure that he would receive bail, not realising at all that fate had other things planned for him; something very dark.

"We will stop at the police station on the way. I want to wash up and change my shirt," said Kamble, who looked tired.

The women heard what he had said and three of them boarded the autorickshaw to relay this news to the group of women waiting at the police station, and further at the gate of sessions court. The police station was just a stone's throw away from the designated court.

Kamble had been under lot of stress as the deputy Chief minister was in town for two days, and Kamble was in the VIP protection force also, so he was not getting any rest. He was juggling these two important tasks. He looked at the watch and saw it was just about 3 p.m., so there was enough time in hand as they had to report to the court at 4:15.

Some 20 women were waiting at the station. They had come prepared to tackle this criminal and were armed with kitchen knives and a deadly concoction as per the guidance of their leader, Asha Patil. Very small, thin pieces of green chilli, ginger, grounded black pepper, mixed with mustard oil, and kneaded into a fine paste.

Initially, they had thought of red chilli powder, but the problem with it was that it flew in the air and the thrower also could get a dose of it. The concoction they had in hand was to be applied in the eyes to give the burning sensation.

As Kamble washed and changed his shirt at the police station, the leader of this group of totally determined women, Deepa, had a hurried conference with the team. She told everyone to be alert as the time for the bail application was approaching fast. Any time, Bhiku would be brought in, his wrists tied up.

Deepa divided the 120 women into three groups. 80 would be in the main party which would attack the rapist in the court compound, 20 would be near the police station to help out in case anything went wrong, and 20 were to arrange transportation to rush back to the slum of the attacking party, once the act of punishing Bhiku was over. Now, all they had to do was to wait.

THE PERFECT PLAN

Inamdar glanced at the wall clock. His Lordship was not in a good mood. He was nursing a bad hangover resulting from his alcoholic splurge due to a huge argument with his wife over household expenses. Since he could not reach a conclusion during the heated argument, he had resorted to go on binge drinking, as if this could solve the problem.

His wife, Sheila, belonged to a business family. Although the Judge belonged to a family of advocates and earned lot of respect in their circle, in terms of income, they were always struggling.

They only had with them the official car, which was allotted to him, but his wife Sheila had always wanted a vehicle for the family. And now, she had set her eyes on the latest sedan from Korea which came equipped with an automatic transmission. However, the price of the said vehicle was way beyond his budget. He accepted that they needed a car, but "why not go for a second-hand vehicle?" was his opinion. Nowadays, even seconded vehicles came with a year's warranty.

Sheila was not interested in his say. She was simply tired of being seen in an old car. "You have some status in the society, for God's sake. You are a Judge and must always be well-presented in the circle we move in. If you can't, then let me speak to my father. I am sure he will indulge me..."

The last remark got his goatee up and made him very upset. "So now you want me to be humiliated in front of my family and friends by proclaiming that I can't afford even a car for the family? Do you think I will accept this?" he snorted.

He also rued the fact that Sheila simply did not understand accounts. They had two children. The older one, Ranjit, was pursuing his post-graduation in Computer Science while Mini, the younger one, was completing her graduation in law, moving in his footsteps to keep the family tradition alive. Ranjit was in Manipal; his tuition fee and hostel charges amounted to almost Rs. 49,000 per month. Mini's college fees and other expenses came to about Rs. 18,000. These expenses consumed a heavy chunk from his take-home salary of Rs. 1.1 lakh.

The balance amount went into household expenses. Luckily as a Judge, he was handed many perks like free housing, free phone calls, and driver's salary which was paid by the government. By the end of the month, they could not afford to save much. But Sheila was simply not interested in listening to his opinions. In a huff, she got up and left, indicating the talk was over as far as she was concerned.

Inamdar polished off two more pegs and went to sleep. It was a fitful sleep and at 8 a.m. with groggy eyes, he struggled to get up. He had a throbbing headache, and his eyes were red. Somehow, he got ready for court after having breakfast and also having gulped two crocin tablets. But the headache still persisted, and here he was in his court room, trying to concentrate on the job at hand. He saw that it was getting close to 4:30 and there were 6 cases still left on the court list. It was going really slow that day. Lawyers on both sides had been arguing and debating in each case as if there were no tomorrow. Some of the lawyers were brilliant, and on any other day, he would have liked rattling swords with them, but not today. He held his head and tried to press it, hoping to get some relief, but to no avail.

He was afraid this headache was actually a migraine attack and would last for a few hours more. He knew he was in trouble and when he reached home, he would just crash out in his bedroom after pulling all the curtains, ensuring no light was switched on, and no noise came in. He had to sleep it out. That was the only way. And of course, at some stage, the bile would come up in his throat and he would have to vomit; something he just dreaded. But he would feel better after the vomit.

There was no way the cases would be heard that day as court closed at 5:00 p.m. Again, he glanced at the clock, just above the mandatory photo of Mahatma Gandhi with his cute smile, who looked even cuter with one tooth missing. He did not linger on looking at Gandhi as the father of the nation would have not approved of his alcohol binge of last night. But he concentrated on the needles, willing them to rotate faster. The clock struck 5 with a bang and Justice Inamdar literally jumped out of his seat, calling the court clerk to push the remaining cases to the next day, and to also ensure that the case of Bhiku Karandikar came up at around 11:30.

The clerk ran up to him and reminded him that the next day, he had to take three depositions at the police station via video conference. "Sir, you had agreed to take the cases of Magistrate Sunder Shetty, who is busy making arrangements for his daughter's wedding. It should take 2-3 hours maximum, so I will post today's 6 cases left out for tomorrow, post lunch."

"That will be fine, but since I am at the police station in the morning, I will listen to the bail hearing tomorrow of the accused Bhiku at 12 noon, sharp. Inform all concerned. There should be no bungling—just make sure."

Kamble had already reached the court along with Bhiku and his police colleagues. The tiredness still showed on his face. He did see many women in the court, which was unusual, but then, as he rushed to the Xerox machine to make copies of his documents to be submitted to court, he forgot all about these women.

As he reached the court, he knew something was amiss and gulped when he saw Justice Inamdar leaving the premises on a trot.

The court clerk informed him that Bhiku's hearing was the next morning at 12 noon at the police station itself. Kamble had to make all necessary arrangements. The police party, with an unhappy Bhiku trailing in chains, walked back to the station. The man had wanted to be bailed so that he and Kamble would have celebrated. But that was not to be.

Deepa saw the happenings and was dismayed. She had

wanted to finish the job once and for all that day itself. But she thought out loud on this and felt that the police station had more space and a good open area from where it would be easier to disperse and escape. The court was too narrow and so many women may feel cramped. So, yes; now, on re-evaluation, the change of plan seemed even better to her.

The women dispersed and all agreed to meet at the slum meeting place at 7 p.m. to discuss and finalise how they would attack Bhiku the next morning.

Some 150 women, tormented by Bhiku some time or the other, gathered at the meeting place.

An effective and doable plan was worked out. The women knew that they only had to tackle Kamble as he would be armed, but then, they were sure that he would not have the guts to fire at them. So, he had to be immobilised. The two constables and the driver of the police van would not attack them in any case. Sub-Inspector Gulabrao with his big paunch was no match for these fit women who had lots of strength from the physical work they did throughout the day. There was not an inch of fat on most of these women.

And since Kamble was in cahoots with Bhiku, he was almost as criminal as the accused. After all, Bhiku would force some of them to go to Kamble in the night where the lusty police inspector would have his way.

Deepa wanted to know which of her slum colleagues had been victims of Kamble. Some 40 hands went up. This pleased Deepa, and soon, the plan was discussed and accepted by all. Deepa laid down a list of what had to be carried with them. Deepa told them to carry a face mask, a small pouch full of the deadly concoction they had all made, and a sharp kitchen knife.

The stage was set. The predator, who had hunted them mercilessly for many years, was the prey now, about to get a taste of his own medicine, and more.

THE EXECUTION

It was a hot, humid day. By 9 in the morning, the city was already like a furnace. The cold *nimboo paniwalas* (lemonade sellers) were going to have bumper sales that day. And the police station would have no air-conditioning for sure, thought the Judge, cursing the day he had agreed to bail the Magistrate, Sunder Shetty, out. But work is worship as it is said, and Inamdar fervently believed in that adage. So, A.C. or no A.C., he had to take the depositions, even though his shirt was already sticking to his chest. And of course, there was the bail hearing of that serial rapist Bhiku, on which he had to pass his judgement.

He hoped that at least the ceiling fans would be working. Sharp at 9:30 in the morning, his official vehicle entered the police station premises and parked next to the Peepal tree. Inamdar exited, telling the driver, "Madam wants to go for brunch meeting with two of her friends. You take her there and wherever they decide to go. But come back here under this Peepal by 12 noon without fail."

His driver Abdul of many years stood at attention,

nodding his head, and confirmed that he would indeed return to the police station at required time. Abdul was well acquainted with Saheb's anger. He knew he would come 15 minutes early.

****

Deepa and friends went over the plans again and started moving out to the police station.

She had divided the women in three groups. While the 40 who had suffered at the hands of Kamble would tackle the inspector, these women were well prepared and had with them 20 feet of strong rope. Deepa also wanted to reach out to them, and she produced a police-style handcuff which was very easy to operate. She picked out Salma, who looked strong and sturdy to work on the handcuffs. Salma smiled when Deepa whispered in her ears on whom the handcuffs were to be used.

Many women in the evening had wanted to have a rehearsal of their movements and also check their speed in doing the entire job.

Deepa agreed and got a few males of Rinkunagar to act as Kamble, Gulabrao and the other policeman as well as the driver. The whole time it took was 4 minutes. That, according to Deepa, was long, and another 3 rounds of rehearsals got the time down to 3.15 minutes. But since the three groups were to work independently, the time would still be less. The women were ready. In Deepa's estimate, they would not take more than two and half minutes and told the women, "We have to leave in maximum two and half minutes. Make sure of this. We should not be caught and detained by the police or Court Marshalls. Very important."

Another group of 40 were to tackle and ensure that the two constables and Sub-Inspector Gulabrao were rendered ineffective and impotent. The main group of 70-odd women were to concentrate on assaulting Bhiku. Everyone knew their role and what was expected of them. They were all charged up, revenge being the sole thought in their minds.

Justice Inamdar in the meantime was sweating it out inside the visitors' room at the police station. He wanted to finish the depositions and the bail application by 11:30–12 noon so he could escape this heat and return to the cool air of the court, or his personal chamber, which was air-conditioned. The severe migraine which had laid him low the previous day had been contained, but there was still a dullness in his head. He was not feeling energetic.

The Judge was well aware of the accused and what Bhiku stood for. And why not? After all, he was a member of the society and did read the newspaper every morning, while having morning tea in his veranda.

He was an early riser and enjoyed the silence as he went through his docket for the day, what judgement he would give in the cases that came in front of him. Before leaving for the court, he made sure that he was on top of his work and had glanced through all the cases.

He was aware of the dubious background of Bhiku Karandikar. Today, the *gunda* (gangster) was to appear before him, seeking bail. That Bhiku was an evil man, who capable of heinous crimes, was a given. Left to him, the Judge would have given Bhiku a prison sentence for life, or even death by hanging. But he was a legal luminary, and he was forced to evaluate the evidence placed in front of him. His hands were tied by the law and could not deviate even an inch.

Justice Inamdar was also aware of the reputation of the police in this area and empathised with the women who had been terrorised by this goon and the police.

The women had started gathering under the Peepal tree by 11:20. They stood in the groups they were designated with. Nothing to do now except wait. In the meantime, at about 11:30, a car came in and parked near the Peepal. The driver in neat uniform went inside to report and inform the manager that the car had come and waiting for the Judge.

Abdul came out and opened all the car windows. He opened the left window and eased his tall body in the co-driver's seat in. He then concentrated on opening the right front door and pushed it out to open fully. It was the hottest in the daytime now, with the clock showing 11:43 a.m. Everyone seemed to be suffering in the temperature that had reached a gruesome 43 degrees outside. The open windows and the door brought some respite to Abdul as he could feel the light breeze. The women waited patiently. Come what may, today or never was the thinking of these brave but helpless women.

As the clock got ready to chime at 12, the police van could be heard rattling its way to the station's gate. As the van swung into the premises, all women became highly alert. The van turned full circle towards the Peepal tree and came to a thundering stop. The group that was to tackle Kamble immediately shot into action. As he was getting down from the van, he could see the groups of women all over the compound, but just shrugged his shoulders, thinking they were perhaps taking part in some *andolan* (agitational protest). By the time he got down and stretched his feet, the group closest to him put on the mask they were carrying and charged towards him. They roughly pushed him down on the ground and started pelting him with kicks and slapping him hard.

"*Arre ye kya ho raha hai? Mujhe kyon peet rahe ho? Kya problem hai?* (What on Earth is going on? Why are you beating me up? What is your problem?)" he shouted.

"*Haramzadiaon, ruko, nahi toh goli chala doonga!* (Stop it, you morons, or else, I'll shoot!)" One of the women closest to Kamble punched the inspector on his nose and could hear it break. Kamble screamed in pain as his eyes started burning. He thought he was going blind as the paste entered his eyes.

"*Aye, bhadwe! Humko nahin pehchana? Jab daru peeke Bhiku ki saath hamara balatkar karta tha to hum achche lagte the aur aaj hum haramzadi ho gaye, saala madarchod!* (You pimp! Don't you recognise us now? You seemed to like us a lot when you tortured and abused us with Bhiku, and now, we are morons for you? Motherfucker!)"

Hearing the loud screams of Kamble and also of the driver and the two constables, many people from the court started running to see what the noise was all about. Even the women were screaming "Mukti, Mukti" as they attacked Bhiku.

On an indication from Salma, this group roughly lifted him and before he could react, started to tie him up with the rope. Salma barged in and put handcuffs on him, one on his wrist and the other on the door handle of the van. He screamed and shouted for help, but no one came. He was rendered immobile, and the women kept on pommelling and kicking him for a minute before they suddenly left, as had been decided earlier. The group had taken only two minutes to do their job. Next, they had to arrange transport to Rinkunagar, while they waited for the second group to join them.

While Kamble was being assaulted, the second group of 40 was doing its job of controlling the three policemen who were inside the van.

A few had gone to ensure that the driver did not come out of the van while the rest, with face masks on, rushed inside the van and caught hold of the two constables who had the police sticks with them, which the women snatched and started to hit them. These two were pushed out immediately. Many women than rushed inside to drag Bhiku outside.

Sub-Inspector Gulabrao was too stunned to react. He had never experienced anything like this. He sat there, paralysed, taking no action as 4-5 women stood in front of him, ensuring he did not get up.

But Bhiku was alarmed as several women caught hold of him and dragged him outside, where Deepa and her group of 70 women waited. As Bhiku landed outside, the stabbing started.

He yelled for Kamble, screaming, "*Arre, Kamble tu ghoda nikal. Goli mar salion ko. Ye haramzadian jo kal tak billi ban ke deti thi, aaj jabrang ho gayi hai* (Kamble! Take the revolver out. Shoot those rascals! These morons who were like scared kittens yesterday, have suddenly become ballsy)."

As the women gathered around and used the paste on his eyes and face, he started getting the burning feeling. Still, he managed to identify a couple of them. He taunted the eldest of the group, Shaku Bai. *"Mere saath maza ata tha na. Aaj bhi teri loonga. Tu jayegi kahan, saali kutti!* (You had fun with me, didn't you? I'm coming for you today, too. Where will you go, you bitch?)"

An enraged Shaku Bai threw the paste into his eyes and stabbed him, yelling, *"Arre tu zinda he nahin rahega. Aaj tera ant hai. Hum sub yam dutni tera khoon chusne aayi hain. Aaj tera vadh hoga bhadwe!* (You are not going out of here alive. This is your end. We are all Yam's angels, and we're here to feast on your blood. Today is the end of your life, you pimp!)"

Deepa removed her mask so Bhiku could see what she was up to. She asked two sturdy women to hold him as she pushed the entire paste in his eyes and then stabbed him in his abdomen, shouting, *"Aaj tere se hum sabko mukti milegi. Iss bhoomi par tere kuch hi pal baki hain, haramzade. Madarchod! Tere atyacharon se aaj mukti hai hamari.* (Today, we will be freed from you. These are your last few moments on Earth, bastard. Motherfucker! We will all attain freedom from your sins.)" The chant of Mukti was picked up by all others. "Mukti! Mukti!" roared the women.

Losing blood now, Bhiku saw a car parked few feet away with doors open and started crawling towards it. The women followed him, stabbing him all the time. A crowd had started assembling, but no one dared to come and try saving Bhiku, whose reputation everyone knew. Some of the crowd actually egged the women on to kill him. By the time Bhiku crawled to the car, Abdul became aware of what was happening, even as the last few women stabbed the serial rapist. Abdul tried to stop Bhiku from entering the car, but to no avail. He just could not get a hold on the body—there was blood everywhere, oozing out from the vicious stab wounds.

While Abdul rushed to the police station and explained to the Judge what had happened, the women led by Deepa fled outside, where many three wheelers were waiting to take them away to Rinkunagar. It had taken just over two minutes for Deepa and gang to do the needful. Bhiku would not survive with stab wounds, gaping holes, which were all over his body.

The first batch of these women had already left for the slum, which was just a kilometre away. In fact, the autos were returning and along with them a minibus also came, owned by a slum dweller who had been apprised of what had been planned regarding Bhiku and wanted to help. He was stunned at what had been planned and was indeed executed with such military precision. He had taken one batch already, and as soon as he returned, the women piled in and fled along with the remaining autos.

And Deepa, along with a few others, walked at a brisk pace. In fifteen minutes after starting the process of taking their revenge, all the women were back in Rinkunagar.

As soon as Abdul rushed in and opened the room where Justice Inamdar was just winding up last of the three depositions, he knew, looking at Abdul, that something drastic had happened, otherwise the driver would never have barged in without knocking.

The Judge ran outside and saw the horrific site of Bhiku half inside the car, oozing blood like a fountain. "Get an ambulance, fast!" he roared. What had happened here? Who had dared to kill a man inside the police station?

"Where is the security? Where is Sr Inspector Kamble?" He heard a faint plea from Bhiku, "Save me, please. I am sorry for my conduct. *Mujhe maaf kar do. Koi mujhe bachalo* (Please forgive me. Somebody, save me)." Judge realised that this man had only a few breaths left. He heard the ambulance siren, hoping that by some miracle, this man would survive. But by the time the male nurse got to check his pulse, Bhiku had breathed his last.

By then, Abdul pointed out to the other side of the police van, and the Judge saw the comic sight of Kamble with some green-coloured substance all over his face and his hand cuffed to the van. He could not believe what he saw. He asked Kamble what had happened. Being inside of the police station, the main entrance was on the other side, and then, too, in a room with closed doors, he just never heard what was going on this side.

"Sir, I was bringing this fellow for bail hearing in your court. The hearing got postponed for today at noon."

"What is wrong with you? How did this murder take place here? Who killed him, and why did you not stop this massacre?" The Judge had many questions, but no answer was forth coming. By this time, Abdul had rounded up Gulabrao, the two constables and the driver and brought them in front of the Judge, who was in a real foul mood now.

He looked at Gulabrao with disgust. "Look at you; dirty shoes, huge paunch and with a two days' old stubble. You look terrible! You should be ashamed to call yourself a law enforcement officer. Disgrace to the police service. You were supposed to bring the accused to the police station. Now tell me exactly what happened here."

"Sir," started Gulabrao, stuttering a bit, "we were bringing Bhiku Karandikar for his bail application case in front of you here at the station. But as soon as the van stopped, 100 women roughly attacked us with knives and some paste which made our eyes water and was very painful. They attacked Kamble Sir also with knives, tied him up and also handcuffed him to the van –"

"You got afraid of women. Who killed this man Bhiku? I want answers. Now, it is 12:30 p.m. I want you to find out who all killed this man. And I want you to bring me the killers by 2:30 today to my court room. Not a minute more. I have to leave today by 3:30. If you do not get me some of the women who were part of this extreme measure, I will put you in the lockup. Take these two constables in your Jeep –"

Gulabrao interrupted the Judge and got himself a glare. "Sir, what about Kamble Sir?" he asked Inamdar, after gathering some courage.

Thundered the Judge, "Let him be where he is! He has been a real disgrace. How could he allow this to happen? He had a revolver with which he could have frightened the women and this problem would not have occurred. No, let him be here for one more hour and then by 2:30 when you get the murderers, you can bring him along my court. And listen; do not come empty handed or I will send you again and again to catch hold of some of these murdering women. I may be back by 4 p.m. if my work finishes early." As he got ready to go to the chambers, he ordered one constable to run and get hold of the court warden and security staff to meet him immediately.

There had been few murders inside a court car park. But those were mainly inter-gang warfare and guns were used. The Judge have never heard of multiple stab wounds and gangs of women becoming murderers so brazenly. But Bhiku had died under his watch. It was he who had wanted to conduct the bail application here in the police station. It was he who was morally responsible. Judge Inamdar realised that as the word spread in the legal circles, he would become an object of ridicule, at least for some time.

He reached his chambers and slumped in his chair, and as he called the peon to put on the air conditioning and ordered some lunch, he couldn't help but reflect, what was the society coming to? So many people were present but had not bothered to stop the women. But then again, he had heard about the purposeful deaf ear turned by the officials. There was simply nowhere the women could turn to.

CHILDHOOD

Twenty Years Ago

Rupesh Gajanan Patil took the last peg of the country liquor named '*Santra*' with lots of ice as he swallowed the potent concoction in a single gulp, resulting in a burp. He had been drinking with some old friends for the past hour and was now thoroughly drunk. Time to go home, or to the hell he called home. He finished off the last spoonful of fried peanuts with a good helping of green chillies. The chillies were the most potent available in the country and were bought from Guntur in Andhra Pradesh by a local dealer. Their potency and bitterness hit him as he tried to stagger out from the country liquor bar. Losing his balance for a couple of times, he finally found his footing, and then, with a typical swaggering gait of a person who was inebriated, started moving towards his house, or actually a shanty, which was just one room in a nearby slum.

Home for Rupesh was a place he would rather do without. The dominating, terrifying visage of his wife,

Rupali, sailed across his eyes. The snarl in anger, the screeching voice, the constant nagging for money, money and more money while berating and taunting him for destroying her life made him quiver with fright and depressive all the time.

The estranged couple had a son, Bhiku, whom the father adored, and often bought small chocolates or toffees for the boy. Bhiku had big, luminous eyes and a charming smile. He also loved his father; his eyes dripped with large tears whenever Rupesh was terrorised by his mother. Rupesh never fought back, nor did he raise an arm at her.

The screaming, shouting, wailing happened almost every night. Rupesh received a salary of Rs. 10,200 monthly for a 12-hour shift, and many a times, the 12-hour would become 24-hour or even a 36-hour shift as the guard who was to relieve him did not turn up. The company he worked for had harsh rules and one of them stated that a post should not be unmanned at any time.

All the pressure along with the sleepless nights and days led to high blood pressure, hypertension, and breathlessness at times or even disorientation. But more than anything else, it was his addiction to alcohol that was creating major problems in his life.

But he couldn't help it as liquor was the fuel that kept him going, and after duty, he mostly trudged over to the country bar for his daily quota. The alcohol did not come cheap, and the result was that he was out of pocket by some 3000 rupees monthly, something the wife could not accept, as she could not manage the house in the amount that Rupesh dutifully plonked in her hand on 10th of every month.

Bhiku's school and private tuition fees along with other expenses amounted to about 3000 rupees, grocery was 5000 for the family, with some extra expenses every month like medicine and clothes cropping up, leaving them with no money. Even the meagre amount that Rupali earned as a house maid from two households of a nearby high rise could not bridge the deficit. The two already had borrowed from friends and were not able to return the same, so that route was out.

She wanted more and she was right, but Rupesh just could not provide anymore. Rupali, the wife, resorted to slapping him around in sheer frustration, but to no avail, as liquor and Rupesh were bound together for life; he just couldn't give it up.

The verbal duels and the physical violence were too much for Bhiku to bear. Though he loved his father the most in the world, he dreaded the time he came home and simply ran out to play with friends. Everyone in the *'basti'* (settlement) was aware of the situation in his house and kids teased him. He could not meet their eyes. He started hating his mother and cursed her every time. He knew that most men in the *'basti'* drank but they, as far as he knew, did not create such scenes in their houses.

Bhiku started becoming a loner, hated going to school or playing with his friends. One day, Rupesh came home early as he had fever and was surprised to see Bhiku at home. The boy had caught a rat and was torturing the poor rodent by pricking it with a sharp needle. "What are you doing, *beta*? Leave that poor fellow alone. If you continue, he will die," said Rupesh in alarm. "And why are you not in school?"

"Baba, I don't like school or even playing here with friends. I like to be on my own," answered the teary-eyed boy.

"But why is that? I don't understand, why no school? Afterall, we are paying your fees," persisted Rupesh.

"Everyone teases me, Baba. They call me the coward son of a coward father. Because you get beaten up by Mai. I hate her. I can't take that now. It is better for me to stay on my own. I want to give up studies; at least you can save lot of money this way and Mai would stop hitting you around," retorted Bhiku. This was something that the father did not want at all. Gently, he tried to insert some sense in the boy's head.

"You have to study, *beta*. You have to study as this is the only way you can crawl out of this wretched life that we lead within these slums. Once you graduate, you can get a decent job. Aspire for a better life, my son. Do you know Uncle Prashant who works with me, but is older? His son is now a salesman speaking good English as well. All because he persisted with his studies. You don't want to end up like me—a loser in life," said Rupesh, wiping away the tears which were cascading on Bhiku's cheeks. "My father did his best to educate me, but I resisted and remained illiterate; and see what happened to me. I will not like you to have a thankless job like mine."

"No, Baba," sobbed the boy. "I will work in the teashop of the slum gate. My friend Ramesh from our *basti* is working there but will leave the job soon as his family is shifting. He earns Rs. 1,500 monthly and gets to eat, too. I have decided, so that is final."

Rupesh knew he had lost the argument.

"Why don't you hit Mai back? Why don't you retaliate like a man? You just keep quiet while she slaps you around. If I was in your place, I would have hit back and probably killed her," Bhiku asked, wanting to know.

"You know, it is not entirely her fault. She is upset because I am not able to earn more money. And I am not able to fulfil her desires."

"What desires, Baba?" asked the curious son. "You work hard and give all you earn to her."

"You will not understand now; you are young. But in time to come, you will. It is all my drinking that is responsible for the mess in the house. Now, one last time, I am asking you to go to school. I will be happy. Do you love me or not? Tell me."

"Of course, I do," said Bhiku. "I love you the most in the world. But I am not going to school." Rupesh sighed and now simply wanted to rest.

Rupali came back from work and found Rupesh soundly sleeping. She wondered why he was home early, and then typically, she started getting angry. As per company policy, his salary would be deducted, which meant less money in her hand for running the house.

Frustration again turned to fore as she screamed and roughly pushed him. "Why are you home? You will lose day's wages, don't you understand? Why did you marry me, idiot? You wanted an *aaya* or *kamwali* (maid or servant) in the house. You have given me nothing."

A harassed Rupesh almost fell down from the bed. He

tried to explain that he was not well and was running a fever, but she would listen none of it. "Get up and go to work, you good for nothing. Even better, don't come back. I will be happy if you die." She was almost frothing from her mouth in sheer anger.

Just then, Bhiku walked in with a smile to inform his father that he would start working at a tea stall after five days. But the smile soon evaporated when he saw the scene inside. He also heard Rupali saying she would be happy if his father died.

Looking at Bhiku, she realised that the boy had bunked school. "What are you doing here?" she started yelling. "How dare you bunk school? Do you want to grow up illiterate like this wretched man?" she screamed.

Bhiku looked daringly in her eyes and told her he was leaving school as he did not want to study further. "I am starting work at the tea stall tomorrow."

Speechless for a moment, Rupali landed two tight slaps on Bhiku's cheeks which sent him sprawling to the ground. A stunned Bhiku got up quickly and eyes blazing with anger shouted, "Don't hit me again. I am not like Father, who does not hit back. You will regret this; I will not take it lying down."

Bhiku then rushed out of the house, eyes brimming with tears which came cascading down his cheeks.

UNEASY TRUCE

Twenty Years Ago

It was not always like this. Rupesh and Rupali had been a happy couple in the early years of their marriage; they had been married now for close to 15 years. Both their families belonged to Ratnagiri and lived almost next to each other in a small village called Vithalgarh. Life was difficult for them as their main occupation was farming. But even then, they were totally dependent on the God of Rain to have a good yield. The farmers toiled hard to grow rice and sugarcane, since both demanded high level of water. Too much or too little damaged the crops. Rainfall had to be just right.

Both the families' survival proceeded from hand to mouth, but they were still content with what they had. The younger generation, however, was not too keen on farming, and many of them were drawn like a magnet to Mumbai, where even odd jobs offered them good enough salaries. In fact, they could save some money and send it to their families left behind.

Rupali was a year younger than Rupesh, and they both went to the one and only school in the village, which was at short distance from their house. They got to know each other while growing up together. Life was real fun for Rupesh as he whiled away his time playing with his friends, immune to the financial problems faced by his father due to the fluctuating duration of rains. He was the youngest in the family with four other siblings and was pampered to say the least.

The games played by Rupesh and his friends were typical rural games like *gulli-danda, lagori,* seven stones, *kho-kho* and the likes, which invariably meant lot of running around. Rupali, too, would join the gang at times.

Both turned in their teens, growing up strong and resilient. Rupesh, however, was not inclined towards studies and decided that his future lay in Mumbai, where two of his brothers had already gone and were working on the construction sites.

His father wanted him to continue his study at least till his 10th standard, but Rupesh was simply not interested. He said school was a waste of time and did not listen to his old man. And by the time he turned 16, his interest lay elsewhere. He started seeing Rupali a lot and wanted to spend time with her. The love slowly blossomed, leaving behind the age of innocence as they entered the age of curiosity, trying to understand and explore their bodies. It was at the annual *mela* (fair) or the harvest time '*jashna*' that they finally got really close to each other.

The mela was real fun and so very colourful with stalls

selling lovely food and games aplenty to play. The *'kaleidoscope-wala'* made brisk business as every teenager was drawn to it like iron studs towards magnet. So was the funny mirrors' stall where you saw your body in different shapes and would die laughing. Then, there was *'buddhi-ka-bal'*, the delicious fluffy, sweet, pink coloured, hair-like cotton candy, handed to you wrapped around a stick. And yes, the spinning wheel or the *'jhula'*; where you went up and down in circles and got really dizzy. It was a mandatory enjoyment for all teenagers.

Since the *mela* happened only once annually, there was no curfew with the timing to return home as far as Rupali was concerned. The two, having eaten their full and enjoying all the games available, did not know what else to do. The evening was still young; it was just descending into twilight. Rupesh had been enamoured by Rupali for some months now and he wanted to share his feelings with her.

Her lilting laughter and those large luminous eyes were a fatal attraction to him. She would smile with ease, just like she was doing now, and her face was illuminated by a radiant charm. She sensed his desire to speak something but lacking the courage to do so from his gestures. She had an idea what he wanted to confess, so in order to encourage him, she gently held his hand.

"I think I am falling in love with you. I don't know how you feel about me, but I definitely want to know you better," he blurted out at once as his face was dyed red with blush.

"I like you very much and I agree to having a relationship with you," said Rupali with a smile as she accepted his cute confession.

The two, holding hands, walked around and found a place which was camouflaged, surrounded by green shrubs all over, and provided them with a sense of privacy. He held both her hands and she willingly entered his embrace, gazing deep into his eyes. He put a hand under her chin and pushed it upwards as he kissed her shyly. She reciprocated with the same intensity as their tongues danced in love. Rupesh was now excited and aroused and his heart started pumping blood faster as he tried to put his hand under her blouse, but she caught his hand and whispered, "No, no. Not now. We have enough time to do all this. Let us talk about our future first."

Rupesh agreed immediately and the two trudged back towards their house after enjoying some chaat which they had missed.

The next 6 months passed by in a haze with stolen moments and lusty kisses. They went to the nearest cinema hall which was ten kilometres away to enjoy the latest movie releases, hand in hand, looking very much like a young couple in love.

One day, Rupesh announced that he would be going to Mumbai in a search for a job and would come back to marry her, taking her away to Mumbai with him. With tears brimming in her eyes, she asked him, "When will you be back? How will I pass away the time now? And promise, you will not forget me. Please remember, I will be waiting for you with a heavy heart."

Their parents had accepted this relationship and just wanted the two to be happy. So, Rupesh had no worries on that account. He promised Rupali that he would first get a job, find a place to live, and would then return to take her away.

In Mumbai, he met his brothers and they helped him to get a job with the same contractor, but he was put to work on a different site. It was backbreaking labour, but he was young and strong from all the activities in his village, thus, he seemingly enjoyed it. At the construction site, the work on the building was about to be completed, and therefore, better security was brought in.

Rupesh saw their nice uniforms, polished shoes, well-built bodies and noticed that most of the workers like him were in awe of the new guards who worked a twelve-hour shift.

Rupesh was now hell-bent into becoming a security guard, and therefore, got friendly with the supervisor. Rupesh was young, strong with rippling muscle, and carried himself with ease and confidence. He realised that the supervisor would help him, but not openly; he asked him to meet him in a bar close by. The supervisor was going to bring another senior supervisor with him. If both recommended his name, then the company would be ready to employ Rupesh.

So, after completing his work for the day, he took a bath, dressed in his best clothes, picked up some 800 rupees which he always kept hidden, and walked to the bar, where he found both already present, and in fact were having their drinks. Rupesh knew that he would have to pay for the drinks and dinner as he had invited the two.

That was the first time he had imbibed alcoholic drinks, and he liked the result. Both his guests promised to recommend his name to be an employee of the company. The evening wore on pleasantly and they parted company around midnight. He was assured of a job and therefore did not mind the Rs. 689 he had to pay for the evening. As promised by the supervisor, the security company called him for an interview and liked what they saw. He was a strapping young man with a pleasant personality and decent manners. He was selected immediately and was offered a comprehensive salary of Rs. 5,500 per month for a 12-hour shift.

He liked his job, felt important in his shining new uniform, and did his job diligently, following all rules and regulations. He made friends from the same community, and the senior ones asked him out to the bar for drinks. He had started to like liquor the first time he had gone with the supervisors. He talked about hiring a shanty close by, so that he could get Rupali to come with him. He was helped by these senior guards, and soon, he had hired a shanty in a near-by slum.

But since he had to complete at least six months in the company before he became eligible for taking leave, he phoned Rupali and gave her the news.

Six months finally passed by, and he was granted a week's leave.

He caught the first available train to reach Ratnagiri, ran from the station to catch a bus for the village, excitement engraved all over his face.

He had saved enough money to have a hurried marriage, bought presents for both families, and was ready to rush back to Mumbai with his bride.

They would live in the city together, go to beaches, visit the big temples, watch movies and even some Marathi theatre. Mumbai's street food became a passion with them; they could not get enough of it. Rupesh had bought a second-hand TV, and once he came home, it became a ritual for them to watch the popular programmes together. Life was really good.

Initially, Rupali found everything great in Mumbai, except that she started noticing that after his shift was over, he did not come home immediately, but came after consuming some '*daru*' on the way. She kept quiet for some months as he always had some reason to go for his drinks.

But four years into the marriage and just before Bhiku was born, she realised that expenses would mount after the birth of their child, and with his salary now of Rs. 7,300, it was not going to be enough. In fact, the initial hospital expenses for delivery would amount to some Rs 8.000, while medicines, doctors' consultation and the rest would almost cost Rs. 2000 monthly for the next three months at least.

Where would the money come from? Rupesh consoled her to not worry as he would be arranging the cash, as the company provided them some loan. Rupali had to run the house and she realised that the drinking expenses of approximately Rs. 1,700 to Rs 2,000 had to be stopped. Within 6 months of Bhiku's birth, the first argument took place. Rupesh promised he would give up liquor but that remained only a promise as he was slowly turning into a certified alcoholic. Slowly, the frequency of fights increased, and as a desperate measure, Rupali turned more and more aggressive. To help fulfil the budget, she started working as a maid, but even that amount earned was not enough. The shouts and screams soon turned physical, continued to this day, unabated.

Bhiku did not return home that night. He found shelter near his school and decided to sleep the night out in that place. The swarm of mosquitos did not bother him. When he felt hungry, he drank from a tap nearby. The early morning saw him dragging his feet towards his house. Rupesh was still sleeping and Rupali was not to be seen. Near the stove, he saw some *roti sabzi* (flat Indian bread with cooked vegetables) kept for father and son. He tried to wake Rupesh up, but he would not get out of his deep slumber. He grabbed two *rotis* and rushed out of the house.

For some time, an uneasy truce persisted in the house. Rupesh was well now, and had re-joined his job, but the alcohol in his life continued relentlessly. So did the scenes at the house. Bhiku hardly spent any time at home. He got his breakfast and lunch at the shop and worked there from 7 a.m. to 6 p.m. Then he rushed off to play cricket with his friends.

One evening, he came home late, and he saw his mother dressed to go out somewhere. She had applied lipstick and powder, which she hardly ever did. And the most surprising element was, she was humming to herself.

THE JUDGE

Present

Justice Inamdar had been in a state of shock ever since he saw the battered and brutally attacked body of Bhiku half inside his car. As he digested what Kamble and Gulabrao had told him, he thought how this ghastly crime will affect his career. To pre-empt any problem, he had sought an appointment to see the Chief of Justice and explain what had actually happened and that he had ordered the murders to be caught and face the wrath of the law. Basically, he wanted the Chief to hear from him first-hand before he started getting gossip rather than actual facts.

Inamdar had never been in this predicament in the 35 years he had spent in this profession and the last five years on the bench as a Judge.

He was just about to sit and order coffee and relish the air-conditioning; he also felt that coffee would ease his still throbbing head when his phone buzzed. Just the person he did not want to talk to right now, but he also knew he had no choice. "Hello, Sheila, can you make it quick, please? I am really very busy right now," he requested, hoping the conversation would not move towards the direction of the car again.

But Sheila, his wife, started off where she had left last night, much to the annoyance of the Judge. She was hell-bent on buying a new car and wanted to contact the dealers for a test drive.

"Look," he said, cutting Sheila off, "I am not in the mood to discuss the car. A murder has been committed right in front of me. I am busy and I have a headache, so just back off and we can debate this car business if I am well enough." Inamdar slammed the phone down, asked the peon to get him a cup of hot, strong black coffee along with a sandwich. He then placed his feet up on the table and closed his eyes, mulling over what had happened and what steps he should be taking regarding the women who had gathered together in the police station and committed such an unprecedented crime.

****

As ordered by the Judge, Gulabrao took the jeep to Rinkunagar along with two constables. Exiting the jeep at the entrance of Rinkunagar's shanties, the three policemen hurried to the small ground inside, where the dwellers met in evenings to trade the day's gupshup.

Gulabrao was huffing and puffing, breathing hard as he tried to match the pace of others, while cursing these murderous women under his breath. He was just four months away from retirement after a 30-year-old tryst with law enforcement. He wanted to have it easy, doing deskwork in the station and collecting *hafta* here and there, but the main issue in front of him was his elder daughter Rekha's marriage. Gulabrao cursed his wife, too, for having borne him three daughters. With his diligent work schedule, he had collected enough money for the dowry and other requirements for his elder daughter's marriage.

Now that this Bhiku murder case was to be sensationalised, he would have no rest, and consequently, his collection of *hafta* would suffer, leaving him helpless with the marriage of his remaining two daughters.

Gulabrao, too, like every other constable, had started off as honest and decent, wanting to work for the society, making sure law was respected and enforced wherever required. Born in a poor family which lived near Chandanpur, surviving almost from hand to mouth, he was one of six siblings, and his father provided for them by tilling a small one-acre farm.

The family consumed half of what they grew and sold the balance in the government *mandi* (market) close by. But since farming in the country depended so much on rains, they would get a good yield of crop only once in maybe 4 or 5 years. More rains, less rains or unseasonal rains destroyed the crops. Then, there were locusts, insects and birds which also posed major problems. So, most years, the family could not gather enough to pay for their expenses like schooling, medical, clothes and what-have-you.

Gulabrao was the second born and he was not able to study much as he was required to work on the farm. He dropped out of school to focus totally on the farm as his father could not execute all the hard work alone.

Gulabrao was also given the extra responsibility of looking after the cows and the few goats the family reared. Due to his hard work and the good wholesome food that he received, he grew up into a tall, muscular boy. It was another matter that most times he would wear tattered clothes and shoes with holes in them.

But a chance visit to the city by the father-and-son duo to buy Diwali sweets changed his course of life. They were passing by the local police station when they saw a poster for the fresh recruitment of constables in the police force. The poster stated, "If you are over 18 years of age, passed 8th standard, are at least 5 ft, 8 inches tall and in good health; then now is the best time to join the police force and serve the society." Gulabrao and his father digested all this, but their minds were made up when they further read a sentence which stated that the monthly salary would be Rs 1,500, and the selected recruits would also be entitled to free housing along with medical services.

They bought the sweets and returned home without discussing what was in their minds; it was only at dinner time that the father brought up the subject.

"Today, in the city, we came across a police recruitment drive. I want Gulab to apply for the 'selection mela' (selection trials) and take his chance. Personally, I think his chances of being selected are high. He will receive a salary of Rs. 1,500 per month, not to mention the other perks. With that, he should be able to send money to the family. Also, since it is a permanent and prestigious job, he will be showered with respect. I heard that 'policewalas' (police officers) get to earn more in the future. So, Gulab, you go ahead; you have my blessing."

An elated Gulab was of course keen to join, and since selections were 10 days later, he decided to visit the police station and enquire about the 'what's and 'how's of the selection process.

The enquiry desk of the local police station was manned by a burly-looking character who told him that he would have to run four laps of 100, 200, 400 and 1500 metres, respectively. There would also be some weightlifting drills, but that was it.

A happy Gulab returned and informed the family of the requirements. Father immediately took a decision that Gulab would not work in the field, nor would he rear the cows anymore. Instead, he would concentrate on the running and weightlifting drills.

By the time the selection day loomed on him, Gulab had diligently worked hard and was deemed fit. He won all the races and was ranked second in the weightlifting competition.

He was sure of getting selected but had to wait for a week or so, as the results were still being collated, after which the leaders would be announced. After all, some 890 aspirants had come and registered for the selections. As he had envisaged, he was not only selected but also ranked on top of the list of the selected candidates.

The recruitment process proceeded with three months of intense training, which included firing with the almost obsolete 303 rifles, understanding the law in a nutshell, hand-to-hand combat lessons and general fitness. During indoor classes, it was drilled in the minds of these fresh recruits that they were selected to serve the society and the nation. Thus, they had to be honest and hard working.

Gulab digested everything and with stars in his eyes, started his career as a beat constable, with a small cane or a '*lathi*' as his only weapon. He was right in thinking that his uniform had enough charisma to strike terror in the eyes of criminals. For a couple of years, he led this disciplined lifestyle, and though he saw that his colleagues were accepting bribes and *haftas*, he diverted his eyes and ignored their misconducts.

He was not privy to a lavish lifestyle of the IPS officers, like the SP or the Senior Inspector in charge of the station, as he was usually on his beat after signing the attendance register and did not know much of what happened at the station.

After two years, he was transferred to the enquiry desk, and it was here that his eyes opened with disbelief at the way his bosses were milking the system. First, he refused to accept any money, but soon, after noticing his colleagues' lifestyles changing with the bribe arriving from under the table, he started having second thoughts.

One night, the senior inspector called him and said, "Coming Saturday night, we are having a New Year's get together at the RimZim bar. You will have to come by 9 p.m.; not in uniform, though. We will see you there," he concluded. Gulabrao saluted smartly and left the cabin.

That party changed his thinking and brainwashed his philosophy. He dearly wanted to be a part of the gang, and this was the night that made it happen.

Cajoled by his fellow constables, he had a beer which made him feel nice and happy. Another beer followed and he felt on top of the world. One of the constables, who was a year senior to him, proceeded to ask Gulab the reason he did not take a little bribe here and there.

"With the low salary we get, it is not possible to live well. Plus, I have a daughter now, and caring for her requires a good amount of money. We can hardly save anything, plus our duty hours are atrocious; still, our salaries remain the same for years. I also started like you, with patriotism in my mind. But seeing no help arrive from any angle, I started taking *hafta* here and there. You know our bosses also conduct business under the table heavily and lead a rich life. So why shouldn't we? You don't have to do anything. The cash just comes to you."

That set the ball rolling. Slowly but surely, Gulab started hinting to some shopkeepers on his beat that they would have to start paying *hafta*, otherwise they could face problems. No one wanted to take *'panga'* (to mess) with the police, and thus, meekly, they started handing envelopes to Gulab.

Then, he came to know that if you wanted more lucrative beats with more shops, more restaurants, and a vegetable market where half the stalls did not have a license and were illegal, then you had to pay to your higher ups in the police station. The price to patrol the lucrative beat was steep, but then, you would recover the amount in a few months, and after that, it was as if you were celebrating Diwali every week.

As he sunk deeper and deeper in the quagmire, he became

more and more corrupt. He could not spend that extra cash openly, which led to drinking at the RimZim bar becoming heavy, and soon, he developed a paunch and puffy eyes of an alcoholic. Alarmed at seeing the deteriorating shape of Gulab, his father insisted that he get married and have a family so that he would be more responsible about his life.

Rekha, the eldest daughter, was born within two years of his marriage, followed by two more girls in quick succession. The expenses started mounting with three children in the house, ranging from their schooling, clothes, medical to many other things.

He was desperately trying to procure money from whichever source possible. He bribed his superiors heavily and got lucrative areas to work in as he shamelessly collected whatever he could. The best was the Octroi check *'nakas'* or checkpoints, where the desperate truck drivers were willing to fork out good sums, so that the goods inside wouldn't perish or get spoilt. Gulab made a killing over here. He was able to save enough to cover the marriage and dowry expenses for Rekha, who was soon coming of age. With his few months' tenure left, he had hoped that he would be able to collect more than enough for his second daughter. As it normally happened in the police force, he was promoted to the post of Assistant Sub-Inspector with a year to go in his service. He was allowed to wear a holster for the revolver he was provided and that added to his stature, and yes, menace.

But now, he was getting embroiled in this useless murder case, and he knew that many days were to be wasted. Alas, he had no choice, as he cursed Kamble again and then moved on with the job at hand.

THE DAMNING EVIDENCE

Twenty Years Ago

Bhiku had decided to keep an eye on his mother, Rupali. He felt something was amiss because she seemed to be meeting someone clandestinely. To find out where she went, he would have to arrive later than usual or head to the place she worked at and then follow her home.

Bhiku confided in his closest friend, Gopal, about what he wanted. Gopal, the son of a ragpicker couple, suffered from a similar problem. His alcoholic father would hit his wife almost every night for no reason. Food was either too hot or too cold, the house was dirty, her clothes were stinking, there was not enough water in the house to bathe, and so on. Any excuse proved to be good enough for him to raise his arm on the hapless woman. Now, this was something that Bhiku had come to respect. When Gopal narrated this fact to Bhiku, the boy started idolising the man.

Why couldn't his father handle his wife the same way?

Gopal was two years older than Bhiku and understood the ways of the world more than his friend. He had a baby brother who was 8 years old. Gopal would cover his brothers' eyes and ears when their mother was being pelted brutally. And late in the night, he would hear grunting noises. Their small shanty only had a dirty curtain dividing the sleeping areas of the boys and their parents.

There was hardly any concept of privacy in these slums, and therefore, children grew up very fast. They saw and understood the amorous encounters of the adults. Gopal, too, did not attend school, but helped his parents with their rag-picking businesses.

Gopal enjoyed Bhiku's company and the two could often be seen walking around hand in hand. He had grown up in the slum and knew it inside out. He wanted to help his friend, and therefore, decided to stalk Rupali, trailing her movements. He worked on his own and was able to find her without any problem. He was aware of Bhiku's problem and in addition, he did not like Rupali, who would shout at him for no reason if he came home to pick up Bhiku for a walk or for some other reason.

"Bhiku, Gopal is not a good boy. He is a vagabond and will mislead you; he does not attend a school to learn better things in life," she would advise, adding that he should keep his distance from Gopal, who in her opinion was good for nothing.

Gopal, true to the plan, waited under a tree some distance away from the location where Rupali worked and followed her to the shanty. He was not upset or impatient when nothing unusual happened in the first 6 days. But he was soon rewarded on his seventh day, when Rupali walked back home at a faster pace. He immediately knew something was up and was sure he had hit a jackpot.

Within 20 minutes, she was out, well dressed and humming to herself. There was a purpose hidden in her happy gait. Gopal noticed that she seemed to be in a hurry and was eager to reach her destination. A couple of times, Gopal was very close to her, but she did not notice him as she walked on, looking down. It was around 7 p.m.; by this time, Gopal had an idea as to what she was up to, and he was not wrong in his thinking. Rupali was almost at the other end of Rinkunagar, where there were some nicely built shacks rented out by local goons, on an hour-to-hour basis. It was a notorious place with a brisk business. Rupali approached one of the shacks, looked all around to ensure no one had spotted her, then calmly went inside.

Five minutes later, an autorickshaw arrived and was parked in front of the same shack. Gopal recognised the face of the driver. The person was Vikram, or better known as Viki; he lived in the slum area next to Rinkunagar and was often plying his auto here. On Sunday mornings, he would even join in the cricket games with a senior group.

Gopal edged closer to the shack but did not want to be seen by the goons running the show.

As he walked past, he heard squealing and grunting noises and soon realised the situation.

Rupali emerged a few minutes later and walked home, looking contented and satiated, buying some green vegetables on her way to portray she had gone shopping if asked by Bhiku, who might be at home. Gopal waited till she entered her shanty, then left to find Bhiku and update him as to what he had just witnessed.

FACE-OFF

Twenty Years Ago

Bhiku was late today. Sunday meant a lot of customers for the tea and snacks that he served. But he was just wrapping up when Gopal rushed in with his news.

Seeing Bhiku about to leave, Gopal went outside to wait, wondering how he would break this news of the amorous tryst of Rupali and Viki to a 12-year-old Bhiku. It was a delicate matter, but his friend must know what his mother was up to. He decided it was better to be straight with Bhiku, instead of beating around the bush.

"Bhiku, do you know what adults do when they are alone? Mostly, they have sex. Your mother has been meeting that auto driver Vikram from the next slum. You know the shacks located at the other side of Rinkunagar, the one you can hire for one hour or so, to secretly with your lover? That is where your mom goes. What will you do about this?"

Bhiku wanted to know what exactly the term 'sex' was but kept quiet. Inside, however, he was seething with anger. He knew a bit that the adults would take their clothes off and proceed to do something. He could not fathom the picture of Rupali getting naked in front of strangers. He thanked Gopal and went to his shanty, where Rupali was busy making dinner.

She was in a good mood and even smiled at the boy. "I am making your favourite '*dal*' (lentil soup) and there is also some chicken for you."

Bhiku smiled but the smile didn't reach his eyes. *I am going to make you pay for hurting my father, once I catch you together with Viki. Just wait,* thought Bhiku.

He took his dinner plate and went to his corner, while Rupali kept on humming some film song. Surprisingly, she was also sweet to Rupesh when he came back home that night. Bhiku wanted to inform his father of the situation, but he first wanted to confirm what Gopal had told him. The problem was how to go and find out what was happening with Rupali, and that person named Viki.

The next day, he walked towards the area which Gopal had mentioned. There were many shacks, and he was not sure which one would be used for the dastardly act. Behind the shacks lay a wall with a good distance separating the front and back of the shack. Soon, a plan formulated in his mind. He would go out of Rinkunagar to the next slum and then climb the wall, landing in the space between the wall and the occupied shack.

Satisfied, he went to work but he knew he had to find out the evening she would leave for her shady business.

He purposely started coming early from the tea stall and taking up position behind the thick Peepal tree. Like Gopal, he was a patient boy, and his patience was sadly rewarded on the ninth day of his stalking.

Rupali came home at a brisk speed and vanished to the public bathroom few metres away from the shanty, and finishing her ablutions, came rushing back. His gut instinct screamed at Bhiku that today was the day for another amorous tryst with Viki. So, on purpose, he went inside to see what was going on. He was not surprised that she was dressing herself in her favourite clothes.

"*Arre*, how come you are home early?" a startled Rupali enquired.

Bhiku just shrugged his shoulders and replied, "I have a cricket match today, so I took time off from work. I will be late." Snatching a T-shirt, he rushed outside, and hid behind the tree to continue his vigil.

Truly enough, Rupali rushed out in a hurry, and started for her rendezvous with Bhiku trailing her at a distance. She reached the shack booked for the day, looked back at the road, and then ducked through the door of one of the shacks. Ten minutes later, Viki arrived in his auto, and much to the amazement of the boy, one more person emerged out of the auto. Without any discussion or time to waste, the duo entered the shack.

Wasting no time now, Bhiku rushed out of Rinkunagar and hurried to the wall area from where he wanted to jump. The wall being a little high to scale, he looked around for some stones, found them, and using them as a step-up, jumped over the wall. Landing hard on his feet, ignoring the pain from his shins, he managed to get behind the shack without being detected. Finding two small holes in one corner from where he could peep inside, what he saw was astonishing.

His mother was almost semi-nude and had an ecstatic look on her face as Viki grunted all over from behind her. It was a disgusting sight and he felt totally helpless, with shame plastered all over his face. Even more upsetting was the person who had arrived with Viki, who had a video camera in his hands and was filming this act of lust and debauchery.

Having seen enough, he jumped off the wall and ran home, his eyes welling up with tears. He was sure he would take this up with his father and see that Rupali was shamed. The mother came in a bit later with some vegetables, which she bought on the way. Around 9 p.m., Rupesh sauntered in an inebriated state as usual. Smiling at Bhiku, he quietly went to sleep, not wanting to have a verbal duel with Rupali, which would escalate into a few smacks from her. But she had seen him walking unsteadily to the bed without eating dinner, feeling good that she had made dinner for the family.

Working up the poison inside her and very upset that the food would be wasted; something they could not afford at all, she barked at Rupesh and shook him out of his slumber, "*Arre bhadwe,* who will eat this food? I don't have a fridge to keep it fresh for the morning. You bring no money and yet you waste so much. Get up, you lazy, good-for-nothing beast! Go and sleep in that *desi bar*. We will manage without you. Get out now before I hit you, you mongrel."

Rupali went berserk and started hitting Rupesh who was still in a daze, not really comprehending as to what had brought forth this sudden onslaught from Rupali. She got hold of a stick and started hitting Rupesh on his behind.

A highly angry Bhiku jumped in between the two and tried to stop Rupali, whose frustration knew no bounds. She did not stop until Bhiku blurted out, "I know where you sneak off to meet Viki and what you do with him, you woman with no morals! I am ashamed that you are my mother. Most people here in Rinkunagar know about you and what you do at that fancy shack. Do you know what they call me? A prostitute's son. Don't touch my father again. Enough is enough! It is you who should leave this shanty. I will take care of my father."

He gently caught hand of Rupesh and told him, "Your nightmare is over, don't fear her anymore. Let's go out for a walk." The duo came back after some time and found Rupali packing her personal belongings. No words were said or exchanged. Rupali just vanished from their lives.

"What did you see, *beta*? Tell me the truth. I want to know and will then decide what to do with her if she comes back. Don't hesitate..."

Bhiku proceeded to tell him what he had seen and finished it by saying, "We will not allow her to come back. You can live in peace. I hate her for what she did to you. She will pay for her misdeeds." But there was a question in his mind which troubled him.

Were all women like Rupali? He had nothing but hatred in his heart for his mother and a woman like her. Was he turning out to be a misogynist, who would start hating women for no rhyme or reason?

THE LEADER

Present

Gulabrao was sweating buckets as his motley group entered that open ground. But to his surprise, it was deserted; normally, it used to be packed at this time. He tried knocking on a few doors, but no one opened. Just then, a constable approached him, waving his hands.

"Kamble sir wants you to find the leader of these murderers, apprehend her and bring her to the station. He also said that you were not to come back till you caught her and few other perpetrators."

Gulabrao cursed under his breath. His *hafta* collection schedule would be hit, and with the Judge breathing down his neck, he was sure that sad days were approaching. Now even Kamble was ordering him around and was rushing to claim credits if things went well, but he would also ensure that all the blame landed on Gulabrao. Not one soul was to be seen at this time. He understood in a way what was going on, but was not too perturbed, since he was certain to get the information he required, through the network of informers he had diligently procured and trained.

He asked one of the constables to run to the tea shop and ask for Amjad. But the informer was nowhere to be seen; neither were Raju, Kapil, Geeta, and his other group of informers. Gulabrao was stunned, shocked in a way, as he had never seen anything like this. Now, he was not sure what to do as not one was opening their door. It was an insult to the policeman. And with his informers being vanished, there was a way. He almost ran to the tea stall with Justice Inamdar's deadline of 2:30 p.m. looming over his head and had nothing to show up with. He had to take some drastic measures. He whispered something to his constables and went inside the stall, straight to the owner, Vallabh. He caught him by his collar and bellowed, "I am arresting you as an accomplice for the murder of Bhiku. You will be handcuffed and taken into police custody for the night."

"What do you mean? I do not know anything about this murder, *Sahib* (Sir), I am innocent," pleaded Vallabh at Gulabrao's feet. But the policeman was relentless with his stand and dragged the hapless man out of the stall.

"*Sahib*, have mercy, I do not know anything," cried Vallabh.

"Then tell me who the leader of these women was, who were brazen enough to kill Bhiku. If you provide me with the correct name and house number, I will let you off. But if you try to be smart, then jail time for you tomorrow is assured. So, fast with the name."

Vallabh had no choice but to blurt out the name of Asha

Patil along with her house number. "But be careful, *Sahib*, she is educated and fearless and has a low opinion of the police."

Gulabrao was charged up and rushed to her house. Asha answered the knock as she waited for Gulabrao to say something. "Are you Asha Patil?" Getting an affirmative nod in return, Gulabrao said, "Then I am authorised to arrest you as leader of the women, responsible for murdering Bhiku," said Gulabrao.

"I see," said Asha, "But where is the arrest warrant? And do tell me, how long have you been in police? No wait, let me guess. I think you are about to retire. But you still do not know that in any case, you have to bring a female constable with you along with a written order from a magistrate under Section 46 in The Code of Criminal Procedure, 1973."

Gulabrao was befuddled for a moment but came back sharply, saying, "All that is theory, your arrest has been ordered by the Judge himself. So, it's better you come along peacefully. I don't want to use force."

Asha agreed to go, but on the condition that they directly go to meet the Judge, and she also agreed to be called the leader of the group of women.

They landed in front of Judge Inamdar just on time. Inamdar was still nursing his headache and thinking about the measures to tackle his wife regarding the car issue. He had decided already that this year had three more months left, so they could order a car early next year, when finances were better. Well, he knew this was at best an excuse and that Sheila would most likely reject it but still had to take a chance.

His current car was good enough to drive Sheila

wherever she wanted to go. Once he was at the court, he was here the whole day, and it was only in the evening that he had to be picked up from the court. In a nutshell, Sheila was just being stubborn and greedy. He hoped she would find sense. This, to him, seemed like a classic case of peer pressure.

Some of her friends belonged to business houses and liked to flaunt their wealth in an obnoxious manner. Sheila, still not being mature enough to understand this, did not appreciate that a Judge's wife was given the respect they deserved by the society, which her friends would never receive. She should be above all these petty things and walk tall with satisfaction and self-respect. When she went for any social functions, people would want to meet and greet her. The type of car she came in did not matter.

It was correctly said, as Inamdar reflected, "It is not the clothes that make the man, it is the man who makes the clothes."

She was being very petulant and must get over her inferiority complex. The Judge sighed deeply and brought his attention back to what was happening in front of him.

Asha, very politely, was telling the Judge that she had to accompany the police under duress. "I was not here in court when this incident took place. Furthermore, breaking all rules and norms these police officers did not have a magistrate order or a female constable with them to arrest me."

Inamdar was aghast, turning red in the face with anger boiling over. He banished Gulabrao from coming into the court at the pain of being arrested. Furthermore, he also fined the inspector Rs 10,000 and ordered a cut in his gratuity and EPF.

"Madam, I am sorry about this, you can go. If any problem arises, let me know," said Inamdar.

Asha thanked the man and left but saw Gulabrao waiting outside. "I know you are the leader; they know you as the snake woman. My boss will nail you." Spitting on the court wall, Gulabrao left for his workstation to report to Kamble. This case had already pained him and cost him dearly, and on top of it, he had to pay the court Rs 10,000. He was upset and distressed.

He would murder the Judge if he had a choice. The next three months looked really gloomy to Gulabrao.

SNAKE WOMAN

From childhood, Asha was mesmerised by snakes. It was inevitable that she took up the study of Herpetology to really understand snakes. She had a degree in the subject. Her love for animals was deeply rooted in her family. She had lived most of her life close to jungles as her father was a ranger in the Forest Department. She had lost her mother when she was about 15 years, and lived with her younger brother and father, taking the role of a mother to her brother and herself.

One day, her father brought a baby python home. The baby python's mother had been killed by a leopard in a fierce fight. Thus, Asha looked after the baby, feeding it small morsels of meat. The baby was also injured in the fight, so Asha had to look after the wound. In due time, the python was released in the wild.

In the jungle, there were many tribes of '*Adivasis*' living there in peace with the animals. They were expert snake catchers. Asha made friends with a couple of these fellows to learn how to catch snakes and distinguish the poisonous ones among them. She was fascinated by the mystery of snakes. They could not hear and everything they perceived was through the vibrations in the jaws. The eyesight of snakes was bleak, which was why their tongues could be seen slithering out in the open.

Contrary to human belief, snakes did not drink milk.

She realised that snakes were not enemies of humans and actually tried to slither away if someone came too close. They attacked only if they felt threatened. By the time she was 16, she had started giving lectures and demonstrations in nearby schools and colleges, teaching kids why and how the snake was not their enemy, and how to appreciate and love these reptiles.

Her father died when she was 18 and with a degree in her hand, brother in tow, she decided to come to the nearest big town where she could find a job. She had to survive, since her father's pension and gratuity amounted to just about Rs 2 lakhs, which she deposited in the bank, and lived off the interest.

To save money, they decided to live in the slum called Rinkunagar, where shanty was cheap to hire with a good water supply. She realised that the slum was full of semi-literate or totally ignorant dwellers, but they were friendly and helpful to her, and that was what mattered.

She registered herself as a snake catching expert with the fire brigade and police commissioner office and got paid Rs 100 for every catch. She was legally allowed to keep snakes at home, but with total responsibility landing on her.

Soon, she was giving demonstration and lectures as before and made a name for herself, earning Rs. 500 per visit, making enough to live well.

Young, well-built Asha may not be good looking, but was attractive enough. She was passable with her fluency in English but knew enough to fill out forms which women in Rinkunagar wanted to fill. This slowly amounted to her being in a leadership role, which she was quite contented to play.

Dwellers came to her for advice, which she was happy to provide. In return, the poor dwellers sometimes brought goodies to eat as a token, which she was happy to receive.

It was an easy, lazy life for her in Rinkunagar, till Bhiku ran into her.

Of course, she had heard about him from various women, but never expected him to be so lecherous, so evil. Victims of rape and extortion regularly came to her for advice. The only advice and the right one she gave was to go to the police and file a written complaint. The raped and brutalised women regularly filed FIRs, but to no relief.

The police, especially, Sr. Inspector Kamble, was in cahoots with Bhiku, and that was that. In fact, going to the police station meant more humiliation and worse, getting raped again and being tormented for a long time.

Since he was on solid, strong ground, it surprisingly took Bhiku too long to zero in on Asha. It was late on a New Year's Eve that he jumped on her with his two henchmen.

CRUCIAL MEETINGS, BHARTIYA NAARI

On that fateful New Year's Eve, Asha had just reached her shanty gate and opened it when Bhiku and his two henchmen waylaid her. Asha screamed for help, but no one dared to come to her aid.

"I have seen you many times but was waiting for the right opportunity to consume you. The question is, will you give yourself up voluntarily or will you resist and fight for nothing?" Asha was left in a helpless situation but would not give up without a fight. She glared at the rapist and spat on him. "I am not a docile victim like the other women you terrorise. You are nothing but a coward, so you prey on poor, helpless women." She had heard some real horror stories about this criminal, and she knew most of them were true.

There were victims of his lust in almost every second shanty here in Rinkunagar, and that he had chopped up a woman to pieces just because she had dared to approach the police station in order to file a harassment report against him.

There were some horrifying stories that stated that one of the victims of his disgusting act was 7 months pregnant, and as a consequence of his inhuman act, lost her baby. One of them was that in order to spread his terror, the one thing that he did most of the time was to rape the victim in her own house.

Suddenly, she realised that her brother should be home or was about to return. He was physically strong and could take on these criminals. So, to attract attention, she started screaming louder and louder.

Bhiku, trying to silence her, caught hold of her neck and tried to tear off her blouse when Asha dug her nails into his cheeks and slapped him hard.

Twisting out of his grip, she turned and caught hold of his crotch, proceeding to squeeze his testicles so hard that tears welled up in Bhiku's eyes. The two henchmen now tried to intervene, when suddenly, the younger brother rushed with a stick and hit one of them hard on his head.

Sensing that the element of surprise had been lost and tables had now turned in favour of the sister-brother duo, Bhiku, with tears cascading his cheeks due to pain, started moving back, but yelling in defeat, "I will see you again, you hell cat, *saali ab to tere ko batana hi padega Bhiku kaun hai* (I will show you who Bhiku is). You have taken enmity with me, which will cost you," squeaked Bhiku, like the criminal he was, still not being able to find his voice.

"*Arre* you *bhadwe,* you won't be able to get it up for some time. Every time you take off your clothes to bathe, you shall remember me. Every time you scratch your balls, you shall remember me. Just don't come near us or I will kill you, you *madarchod* (motherfucker)."

An incensed Asha hurried into the shanty and carefully locked it from inside. She had to be careful with Bhiku. He had tasted defeat probably for the first time in Rinkunagar. He would wait for the right time to avenge this humiliation; if there was one thing she understood about criminals, they had an inflated ego and reputation to protect.

She listened to the women more closely now, and assured them that at the right opportunity, they would make him pay for his crimes.

Asha started making a list of the victims along with the way they were molested. At least ten times that was the count of Bhiku being taken into custody for his crimes when some brave woman filed an FIR, but the court never found enough evidence to nail the hammer down on his actions. As a result, he was always released on bail. He had bribed each and every person present in the chain of command. A night at the local police station *'havalat'* was like a picnic party, followed by wine and women, with Kamble and Bhiku enjoying themselves to the limit.

And when he was released, the first thing he would do was to search that woman out, catch her unexpectedly in her shanty and sodomise her again. The sentries standing outside ensured that he was not disturbed. This modus operandi of Bhiku made sure that the victims suffered in silence. Every second dwelling in Rinkunagar had a victim of sorts. Bhiku's circle of crime also included extortion. He never worked but somehow, he always seemed flush with cash. Each and every shopkeeper was forced to pay him *hafta*. If they did not, then the wrath of Bhiku would land on them. The defiant ones were publicly spanked and if they had a young wife, she, too, had to pay for her husband's bravery by being made an example. The evil named Bhiku had no boundaries.

Anyone dressed in a skirt or saree was potential victim. So, a 60-year-old grandmother, Shaku Bai, was a victim and so was her 12-year-old granddaughter. His brutality depended on his mood and the testosterone level at that moment in his body.

A woman like Deepa, little fair and with a buxom figure had been caught as a fancy subject of his savageness at the very first sight. He had followed her home, stalked her for a few days to know her itinerary and the time she would return to her house.

He then arranged for her to be kidnapped, and his henchmen picked her up like some broken rag doll as they faithfully brought her to his abode. Without much ado, he had proceeded to push her on his bed as he forced himself in her, plundering her spirit and body alike. The screams emanating from her throat did not bother him, as the slum dwellers knew his character better than anybody else.

This very night, about 40 victims had assembled at the shanty of Asha, in order to decide their next course of action that would put an end to this horrifying evil. She was acknowledged as the leader of these women for three sole reasons. First, she had fought against the evil tormenting their souls ferociously, and second, she was the only woman at Rinkunagar with a formal degree of education. Finally, the third and most important reason, a reason that was responsible for the charisma that oozed out of her subconsciously; her quality of fearlessness or in other words, '*nidar*'.

"We are here to protect our dignity. All of us have been terrorised by this criminal, by this animal. We must find a way to finish him off. Do share if you have any suggestions," proclaimed Asha, rousing up the morale of the group and igniting a spark of fighting spirit within them.

One woman stood up and shared her thoughts, "Three days back, I approached our MLA's office for a job vacancy in the party's office. When I informed him I was from Rinkunagar, he asked me if things were normal, to which I immediately answered with a no, and proceeded to tell him and other party workers that Bhiku's terror seemed to know no end, all thanks to support he gets from police and other authorities. The MLA refuted such a claim by straightaway naming it as an absurd notion and that we were being too delusional. He even had the temerity to add that Bhiku had a lot of respect for the '*Bhartiya Nari*,' (an Indian Woman) just like they had in their party and personal life. He further went on to say that he had two daughters and he found nothing wrong with the society." This statement triggered the inner rage hidden within the hearts of the women present.

One of these women yelled, stating that the police was also hands and gloves with him. She continued, "When we go to file a case against him, instead of writing the words that were being spoken; the police, in order to please the media would file a nonsensical case that would name him as a trespasser, or some man spewing abuses and threatening us. This really has no meaning. We must do something concrete," Deepa yelled at the top of her voice, ranting her feelings that were submerged in rage and sorrow for a long time, "*Saala harami* (Bloody Bastard), this Rana Patil. Does he even know what goes on the streets? Not a single day goes by without someone pinching my back or squeezing my breasts. Travelling in the local bus is another nightmare. The man behind you is always prone to bending forward trying to rub my hips with his hardened penis..."

Asha, too, pitched in, "There are close to 34,000 victims of rape in a year all over India and thousands of these cases are devoid of an FIR status as the victims are afraid of the local police, and the lecherous lawyers, who ask the most intimate questions that adds on to the humiliation."

An angry Fatima agreed with Asha as she blazed in anger, "In my case, the police and the defence lawyer painted me as a prostitute, proceeding to question about the times I had sex. Since they were convinced of my identity belonging to someone from the streets, it was me who was responsible for shaming a nice man like Bhiku, who had no proof of conviction as a criminal in the past. But the most annoying and personally shameful was the vaginal test to determine my activity. If the law authorities are so shameless, then which woman can be safe? '*Nari*' has been crumbled under the weighty feet of '*Bhartiya Mard*' (Indian Man) and the dreadful loopholes of the law."

Shaku Bai added her own input, "All these bastards worship the '*Devi Mata*' (Mother Goddess) all over the country. Yet they harass the same female form of her in the night. I hate being a woman in this country..." She sobbed as her already old spine bent further in defeat and despair.

Deepa, though, would not be easily quietened. "I say, every festival that we celebrate is actually a form of insult to 'Nari'. Why is 'bindi', 'sindoor' (vermillion), 'nathuni' (nose ring), 'mangalsutra' (a necklace-like accessory worn by women as a sign of being married), fasting on almost every festival only for us? These bloody men dictate everything for us. Worst among them being 'Karvachauth', fasting for the longer lifespan of these men. We are derogated as 'paraya dhan' (in laws' property) right from day we are born. Even our parents disown us from the moment we are born."

By this time, everyone wanted to have a say. 'Nari' bashing was a hot topic. Shaku Bai, having dried her tears wailed, "These bastards have mothers and sisters, but they tend to forget what will happen to them if they suffer like us. They are all motherfuckers..."

Another chipped in, "Arre, I was not allowed in the Shani temple because I was 35 years old. The Pandit said that no woman between the age of 15 and 55 was allowed. This is strictly followed as they don't want the inner sanctum to be dirty. They turned me away as if having periods is a shameful thing. We must fight all these nonsensical thoughts. In many houses, menstruating females cannot even enter the kitchen. *Inn saale mardon ko paida kisne kiya? Humari kokh se nikalte hain aur usi ki din raat beizzati karte hain.* (Who do they think gave them birth? They insult the same women in whose wombs they were nurtured and grown.)"

Deepa added, "*Ye haramzade janate nahin kya? Agar aurat ko mahina nahi hota toh ye paida hi nahi hote.* (Don't these bastards know that if a woman hadn't menstruated, they wouldn't be born?)"

Asha summed up emphatically as she concluded, "If you think about it, Indian women are their own enemies. Even though a child's sex is determined by the sperm of the man, a man blames his wife for giving him daughters, whereas the men should be the ones blamed. A mother never differentiates between a girl or a boy, as she has carried them both in her womb for nine months. This discrimination leads to female infanticide. Indians want only sons because they bring in dowry. A girl child is considered as a burden. If there exist twins of both sexes, then more often than not, the boy would be the one to get a better diet in terms of quality and quantity both. This mindset has to be changed, but nothing is happening."

They brooded over what was being debated and realised that the sun was about to descend into the horizon as they started dispersing. However, it was left to Asha to come up with a plan that demanded drastic action. It was now '*aar paar ki jung*' (do or die) with Bhiku.

THE FATEFUL DECISION

After hearing the soul-scorching stories of these women and being aware of the fact that Bhiku could strike against her anytime, Asha had become very cautious while venturing outside her shanty. But in a unique way, she had started to arm herself, though nothing was visible except for a bottle containing a white liquid; the bottle which was hanging from her waist.

Thus, an armed and satisfied Asha would go looking for work. She was right in thinking that the rapist must be preparing to attack her, thus avenging his humiliation at her hands.

Asha used to pray at the local Hanuman temple on Tuesday and Saturday evenings. Then, she would buy some groceries on her way back, reaching home around 7 p.m., when it would start getting dark.

On one such fateful Saturday, as the slum was buzzing with activity, Bhiku and his gang of four had stealthily approached her from behind; she was around twenty metres from her door as they sprinted with great might and caught her five metres short from her shanty door.

Asha immediately understood what was happening and started screaming to attract attention. This time, she was totally alert as she turned to face the perpetrators while her left hand whipped out the bottle from her side.

"Come, come, you cowards. You motherfuckers let me see what you are made of. You, *saala* Bhiku, you come first. Don't you remember the kick in your balls from last time? You want one more?" She continued to taunt the pervert.

Smirking, Bhiku snarled his lips, "I have come to enjoy your body. You *saali* (rascal), this time there is no escape for you. I will relish your backside for sure today, *bhadwi*." As Bhiku growled like a maddened animal licking its wound, Asha had opened the bottle with Bhiku totally unaware of her intentions.

Asha threw some liquid on the ground where it started sizzling. "One step more and I will throw this on you. This is acid and it will burn your face, leaving it scarred for life." This was a check mate, and with a crowd gathering to watch the *'tamasha'* (dramatic scene), Bhiku was getting angry and restless. The man behind him had a long stick which he suddenly caught hold of, and with all his might, it hit the bottle. Asha was in agony as the stick had hit her wrist, but this action led to some liquid popping out. The droplets from that spilled acid had landed on the exposed hand of Bhiku. Yelping in pain, the drops started burning his hand, he jumped forward trying to catch her shirt.

"You will not escape today, you slut. Peacefully give in to me otherwise I will kill you."

By this time, Asha had turned and twisted her body and

now was out of reach from the man. She was getting herself in position to catch his crotch again. Alarmed, Bhiku hastily stepped back, giving her some time to reach into her right pocket as she whipped out a foot-long black snake. "Come, come, show me your strength you pathetic man, you *na-mard* (sad excuse for a man). This snake's bite will poison you in a minute, making you paralysed; come, come you coward!" she yelled and started swinging the snake in round movements. In that confusion, Bhiku tripped and fell on his knees.

Now that she took the battle to them, just like dogs, with their tails between their legs, henchmen backed out, leaving a stunned Bhiku alone and defenceless. The hissing snake, with its tongue in and out, was a breed of rat snake, but such was the fear in minds of human beings, making us mortally afraid of reptiles and categorising all snakes as poisonous. Bhiku and gang were no exception to this rule.

A paralysed Bhiku was so hypnotised that he could not utter any sound and simply glared at the snake, now brought dangerously close to his nose by Asha.

"Shall I make him bite you? This cobra's poison will hit your nervous system in minutes, and you will die within one hour. That is guaranteed. So, make your choice. Do you want to die, or will you promise to not trouble me again? Tell me now. And before you decide, make sure that you never lay a hand on any woman from Rinkunagar."

A sweating Bhiku, petrified with fear, swore he would change. "I am very sorry, sister. I will change and will not trouble anyone anymore. Just forgive me."

"Okay," said Asha as she replied, "Now crawl out to the

road and go vanish from our lives."

The criminal crawled and the gathered crowd applauded with glee, seeing the sight of Bhiku on all fours. It became a topic to discuss for months, and Asha became a much-respected heroine instantly. She had the courage to challenge Bhiku, which no one else had.

For some time, there was peace in the slum, but it was just the calm before a storm named Bhiku would rain calamity, just like a dog's tail that could never be straightened unless placed under restrictions.

He struck again, raping a girl of 16 years of age and an alarmed Asha called for a meeting to discuss their next move.

The women then decided to file an FIR and then waited for him to be brought to court. "This time, we must kill him. Enough is enough," they bellowed angrily. The method was discussed, and consensus was achieved. Deepa was happy to be in-charge of the attempt to silence Bhiku once and for all. She swore that he would definitely meet his maker. The fateful decision was made. There was no going back, they swore.

But the question that Asha wanted an answer to, was simple. How had the roots of evil sprouted within him, turning him so violent? What was the reason for his hate towards women?

ATTRACTION

Some 15-16 years ago

By the time he turned 16, Bhiku had grown into a tall, well-built boy, not willing to participate in the different games that the young teenagers of Rinkunagar had the pleasure of playing.

As dusk started descending and cold winds blew from the east to west, he trudged his way home.

He was all alone now, having lost his father two years ago to liver complications, resulting from his heavy drinking. He was now a deputy-manager-like figure on the tea stall and had done successful recce in the meantime to scout out a good location to set his own tea stall up. He was earning well enough, collecting almost Rs 5000 from salary and the tips he received. He had seen his father struggling and fighting against the damage occurred to his liver and had looked after him like a dutiful son. Rupesh had breathed his last in the warm but trembling arms of Bhiku. The boy was all alone now, happy to work overtime so that he could add more money to his kitty, which was swelling up nicely; the saved money was to be utilised for his own tea stall. And since he was not interested in girls, he could save as much as possible. The neighbourhood boys teased him, but he was not bothered.

As the other boys of his age chased girls morning and evening, he remained aloof, not bothered about his monk-like state of life. There was one girl, however, he would look twice at, to show his interest. Ira was also 16 and was the sole breadwinner for her family. She also had given up on school to aid her sick mother, who was suffering from the dreaded breast cancer, a disease common amongst the poor strata of society. Her father was jobless but still tried to earn some money as a *'bhangar-wala'* (junk dealer), picking up unwanted items from people for a small sum and then selling the same at the *'chor bazaar'* for a few rupees more. But then, most of the money he earned went into buying liquor.

She had to work wherever she could; her buxom figure, however, attracted unwanted attention. His testosterone was hitting him suddenly. Alas, she was also noticed by Viki, much to annoyance of Bhiku. He did not like this; thus, he devised a plan to meet and impress her.

Taking few days of leave from work, he stalked her in order to understand her movements. He found that every second day, Ira would go to a place where one was taught to dance on Bollywood songs; with all the *'jhatkas'* and *'matkas'* (sways and grooves).

Bhiku was really smitten by the vivacious girl but could not summon enough courage to bump into her. Then, an idea struck him; why not join the dance classes himself to talk to her, shortening the distance between them?

The very next day, he did just that, but was careful not to befriend her on the very first day, as he thought their first meeting should seem accidental. A couple of sessions later, he saw her eating '*bhelpuri*' (a snack) just outside the dance class and realised this was the moment of reckoning for him, the ideal situation to meet her.

Walking to the stall, he ordered one for himself as he looked at her and smiled. She smiled back, and his heart raced like wild horses.

"I saw your dance today, you really move well, very natural. I wish I could do that as easily as you do," was the opening dialogue. Ira looked up while eating, thanked him, and quickly walked away from the stall.

He did not speak to her in the next two days, biding his time for the next accidental bump. While he was not basically interested in movies or dancing, his well-built body had a rhythm and took to dance easily. The owner and teacher of the class told him to wait after class one day as he wanted to talk to him. So, while the rest of the kids walked away, he stayed put, and to his surprise, he saw Ira also waiting, as the teacher had asked her as well.

"You two are learning well, that is why I am selecting you to have a dancing competition against first-year dancers from a dance school in the neighbouring '*basti*'. It is a friendly match and will be fun. We have ten days to prepare, so let's get down to it. Stay back after class for some special and extra practice."

Bhiku was thrilled. The time after 7 p.m. suited him well

as he would be finished with work around that time and a quick five minutes' walk was all that was needed to bring him to the school.

A couple of days later, it rained, and not having an umbrella, both got stuck under a tree. He asked her where she lived and offered to walk with her, which she accepted.

Then, it became a routine, and he walked her home almost every night. He was at ease with her, and so was she. She coyly asked him one day if he would come to see a movie the next evening with her. Bhiku was of course interested. He dared to hold her hand in the dark theatre and was happy when she did not pull away. His heart was thudding now as he clasped her hand. Leaving her home that night, he became brazen enough to steal a slight kiss.

They won the dance match against the opposition in front of a godly crowd which included Viki, but since the auto driver was sitting in a corner, he was outside the area of his vision. Bhiku and Ira were just so happy at the outcome to worry about anything else.

He had come close to her and realised that at age 16, he had fallen in love with Ira, lock stock and barrel. Women were not so bad after all, and he was even willing to forgive his mother for her behaviour. Days passed with the distance between the two teenagers shortening. He met her parents and visited them often.

And then what was bound to happen, happened. She took the first step and invited herself to his place where she kissed and caressed him. He was out of breath but did not know what to do next. Again, she displayed her boldness as she caught hold of his hand and placed it gently on her breast. She waited for him to fondle her, but Bhiku froze as an image of his mother in that shack hit him and he simply collapsed on the floor, crying.

"What is happening to you? What is the problem? If you are not up to it, forget it. We can do this next time. No big deal. Come on, let's get out if here; let's go for a walk," she coaxed him. But he was still sobbing. Then suddenly, he got up and ran out of the shanty, running in any direction with no destination.

Was something wrong with him? Dire thoughts hit him. He had heard stories from his friends about their encounters with girls. In slums, children basically grew fast physically and mentally as there were hardly any inhibitions, and since most of the time they were left alone with both parents working on daily wages, the post-puberty kids were thrown in each other's company and they would start getting intimate, trying to experiment with the bodies of each other.

Bhiku had avoided all this, though; he had noticed his body behaving differently when a well-endowed female walked past.

Gopal explained to him what was happening and what was needed to be done. "I know your problem with your mother. But you have to grow out of it. There is life beyond. We boys naturally get attracted to girls and they to us. We get intimate and that intimacy leads to sex. Nothing wrong with it. So, enjoy while you can and wherever you can..."

But Gopal did not explain what sex was exactly. He only said, "There is nothing to explain. It will just happen. Don't run away from it, just go with the flow."

But here he was, he had run away, freezing, and not knowing what to do. How would he face her and what would he explain to her when they would meet at the music class? Bhiku actually missed the class, not wanting to face reality. He avoided her when he did go a few days later. It was again Ira who took the first step, walked up to him, and took him in a corner, enquiring about his well-being.

Still embarrassed, he mumbled something insane, but she persisted and said, "Don't run away after class. We will go to your place and talk," she winked.

THE BETRAYAL

The two teenagers, Bhiku along with Ira, reached his place and as soon as he closed the door, she was all over him. Kissing him, cajoling him, coaxing him, gently trying to put him at ease. It did look as if she was in a hurry, but she was so consumed in getting him ready and in a good frame of mind, that she did not notice Bhiku getting a bit agitated. He wanted things to be done slowly, so he could ease himself into the act by first exploring her magical body.

But a fully aroused Ira just wanted him inside her as early as possible, with him on top. Unfortunately, while trying to open his zip as she wanted to feel his aroused member and guide him to the right place, understanding that this was his first time, she did not realise that Bhiku simply had no idea how to go about it.

And as he started to freeze all over again, she now just wanted sex to happen quickly, and was moaning in anticipation, scratching, and softly beating his chest.

Bhiku pulled away, disentangling himself from her, sweating and nervous, wanting to berate himself for not being able to consummate this liaison. "I am sorry, I can't do it, I need more time," he sobbed and left a frustrated Ira behind, who was now trying to please herself with her fingers, moaning away to reach that ecstatic zone.

Ira had been in a physical relationship with a boy next door, but the affair had not been serious, yet she slept with him a couple of times. She was, however, really interested in Bhiku and wanted their relationship to bloom. She soon realised that there was something wrong with him. He was surely not impotent, as she felt him harden on her touch. The reluctance seemed more mental and due to ignorance, rather than anything else. Maybe she was hurrying him, and he was not ready; he wanted to go slow, trying first to get over some demons in his mind. She felt she had to try once again, this time really slowly, letting him dictate the pace and the proceedings. If he failed again, well… then, she had to give their relationship a serious thought.

Unable to concentrate on anything, Bhiku became a forlorn figure for some time, not knowing what to do, but then he decided to confess to Gopal, asking his assistance in order to find a solution to this huge problem confronting his mind. He also decided to cool off his relationship with Ira for some time and therefore dropped the idea of going to dance school for a few weeks. Both of them used Gopal as a courier to pass messages to each other.

He was concerned when Gopal brought the news of her father falling down while drunk and fracturing his hip. And that for this extra burden on family finance, Ira had to quit the dancing school and join the ladies bar close by as a dancer. The bar itself was illegal, but then a good *hafta* ensured it was not troubled by the local police.

Bhiku was aghast, as the ladies bar was a real unsavoury place with a very notorious reputation. He understood why she had taken such a drastic step, but she could have asked him for help; considering their relationship, he would have surely helped her financially. Did she not see that despite what had happened between the two of them, he was actually in love with her? They had been together in whatever sort of relationship they had, for almost a year. He was almost turning 17, but definitely knew to look after himself. And ever since he had started his own tea stall, he was making a good amount of money. He decided to confront her immediately and marched towards her shanty.

"What is the problem with you? Why did you have to go and join that bar? I am making good money and would have given enough to you to tide over this crisis. Come on, tell me what you need," he wanted to know.

"I don't need any favours. I can look after my family. The expense of my father is not just for a month or so. I need Rs 2500-3000 extra per month for his operation, hospital expense, consultations, wheelchair, etc. Plus, whatever little he could earn on his own and gave to the kitty, which amounted to around Rs 1500, is also over. Will you help us with Rs 5000 monthly? No, you can't do that. I am earning good money at the bar, and I will soon make more in tips once I get to dance in first line."

"I don't like the sound of this. You will earn with dubious methods, but you will not take a respectable job. I don't like what you are suggesting."

"Who are you to tell me what to do or not to do? You don't own me," Ira retorted. "I will do what I have to do. I don't need your advice." Ira was under a lot of stress.

Bhiku stomped his feet in anger and rushed out. He liked her so much and was upset that she was totally unaware about the waters she had stepped into in order to fulfil her financial needs. What could he do more, rather than to ensure that she stopped going to the bar? He did not know.

But then, a thought entered his mind. Why not first go to the bar and find out for himself what happened there? So, with Gopal in tow, Rs 500 in his pocket, he set out for the bar on a Saturday night when it was supposed to swing loudly.

The atmosphere was garish, the air thick with smoke, and loud music hitting one from all directions, making it very difficult to hear what the person next to you was saying.

On a stage in the middle of the bar, few very scantily dressed young women were gyrating with gusto to the tunes of Bollywood songs.

Some patrons were throwing currency notes at the women. Most men seemed to be drunk and another group of women acting as waitresses were filling up their fast-depleting glasses.

People were getting raunchy and openly touching the waitresses here and there. The girls, whether squealing in joy or despair, was difficult to know. The dancing girls were now slowly approaching daringly forward and close to the patrons who were now trying to push currency notes in the upper garment of the dancers.

There were three to four bulky-looking bouncers who were tasked with the job of ensuring no one overtly fondled the girls.

The girls danced for an hour or so, and then vanished behind the stage, only to be replaced by another group of girls. Ira came on as Bhiku and Gopal watched in amazement. She was the newest entry in the ladies bar, yet to make her mark, yet to be noticed. But her seductive figure coupled with her ability to dance, which she learnt assiduously in the dancing school, was being noticed by some patrons, who demanded more from her. The patrons now included a known face which Bhiku knew as Viki's and hated him on sight.

He saw Viki trying to get her attention by screaming her name over the din in the bar and then making lewd gestures, at the same time throwing notes at her.

Bhiku got really upset and tried to look away. Gopal sensed that his friend was about to get aggressive and tried to steer him away from the stage. In the meantime, Viki lurched into the stage, trying to pounce on Ira even as a bouncer started to move towards the area to diffuse any violence that may erupt.

As Ira stepped back in haste, Bhiku had jumped onto the stage, rushing to protect her and at the same time catching the auto driver by his neck and slapping him hard. A fight erupted as Bhiku was yelling her name, demanding that she leave at once. Surprisingly, Ira refused to budge, hid behind the bouncer, even, as Viki was trying to get up. And the bouncer, getting directions from the owner, caught hold of Bhiku and was shoving him towards the exit door, when Viki came charging in to land a punch on the boy. But before he could do so, Gopal had stepped in and kicked Viki on his backside. Another bouncer had joined in, and the friends were kicked out the main door of the bar. Humiliated and beaten, they limped towards their shanty.

Bhiku was shaking angrily and wanted to go back to the bar and sort things out with Viki, teach him a lesson. He was also much perturbed by the fact that Ira had not responded to him, even though he had tried to come to her rescue. He had to know why Ira had overlooked him in favour of Viki.

So, he did not go home but instead walked to her house, plonking himself behind a bush, awaiting her return as he wanted to sort out her feelings.

Ira came home around 12 at midnight in an auto driven by Viki, pecked him on the cheek and waited for him to drive out before turning to her shanty, even as Bhiku rushed towards her.

"Ira, I need to talk to you now. Why did you not leave the bar and come out with us?" he demanded. She was red with anger and retorted, "I have recently joined there, and you want me to get kicked out from the job? I told you that you can't feed us, so why are you creating problems for me?"

"But it is a cheap place, and you will soon be forced to do things cheap women do?"

"How dare you judge me and declare that I may do cheap things! How dare you come barging in and destroy a good atmosphere I was building up with a patron! Do you know how much tip I have lost today, you idiot? At least Rs 500. I don't want you coming and harassing me; you don't own me."

"No, no. You are mine. I love you. Please don't do this to me. You don't know how cheap a person like Viki is, he is a real scoundrel who will destroy you after using you."

"Stop interfering in my life. We had two chances of getting really close, but you were not up to it. Learn to grow up, be a man, then come to me. Now go, run, and don't trouble me anymore," Ira concluded.

"You will not stop meeting Viki, you will not stop dancing there, you are hell bent on destroying me and my feelings for you, you cheap slut!" He pushed her hard, trying to be physical now. There was blood in his eyes, and he was not thinking correctly. Ira got up fast from the ground and slapped him hard, "Bastard, get out of my life. Let me be." Sobbing, she ran into her house.

A stunned Bhiku pulled himself up and staggered towards his place. Shaking with anger and helplessness, he walked blindly, and the only thing that flashed in his brain was that he was betrayed. He wanted her as his life partner, and she had betrayed him for someone he disliked, just because Viki was flashy. He could not think properly and just fell down on the bed, now crying loudly. He thought of committing suicide as life had no meaning left now.

Slowly, he took control of himself, thinking now hard how to get revenge.

He would not allow this insult, this ultimate humiliation, to go unanswered. His heart was burning now, and there was only one thought in his mind. How to hurt both Viki and Ira? The future did not matter. You simply could not trust women. His hatred now, for women in general and Ira in particular, was overwhelming. The circle was complete. He would henceforth use and abuse them as much as he could. He would terrorise them and would be known as woman hater now. With these absurd thoughts he finally dozed off to a troubled sleep.

REVENGE AND PUNISHMENT

Fourteen Years Ago

Unable to concentrate on anything while feeling low and depressed, the thirst for revenge propelled Bhiku's mind to think dramatically. The moral strings binding his consciousness were stretched too thin as thoughts on how to kill Ira and Viki remained paramount in his subconscious. He woke up with a splitting headache as his footsteps staggered around a bit, before daring to eat breakfast and stabilising himself. Only then did he begin to calmly focus on the matter at hand.

A pure desire to catch them together welled up in his heart, and the only way he could achieve that was to closely monitor their movements. With that in mind, he found himself at a vantage point capable of observing both her shanty and also the bar. It would take him many days, but he was patient like a predator, striking only when absolutely sure.

Ira hardly left her place during the day. She visited her

work at the bar around 7 p.m. and returned by 11 at night. The only exception to this schedule was on Saturday when her work time was extended to midnight. She would trace her steps back home at nights, except Saturday. It was on one such Saturday, when Viki dropped her home in his auto. They kissed and caressed each other without an ounce of fear, groping passionately before Ira disengaged from him and entered her shanty. One night, she swayed and staggered a bit as if inebriated. The symptoms of a person drunk on alcohol. But, in a detached manner, he, the predator, watched the actions of his prey and remained as calm as a meditating Buddha, plotting and planning his scheme of revenge.

One night, Ira did not return until 2 a.m. at night, but he was still not perturbed; his mind had an idea of where they would have been. Next time, when she did not return by 12:30 a.m., he walked briskly to the shacks; the very same location he had caught Rupali, his mother. Lo and behold, he found Viki's autorickshaw parked in front of one of those shacks. He slowly crept close towards the door as his ears picked up the debauch voices brimming with heavy grunts and moans. His lips curled upwards as an evil grin was plastered on his face. Achieving his goal, the predator returned to his shanty. By the grace of the Gods above, he would soon have his revenge.

A hammer was designated as his weapon of vengeance. Then, a mischievous thought parked itself within his mind. He smiled. Yes, that would be a befitting reply for what she had done to him by rejecting his feelings.

With everything ready now, he lay in wait in his hiding

point, and just as she passed by, he, the predator, pounced on his prey, snuffed her voice, and dragged her behind the bush which acted as his vantage point to spy on her. She, the prey, was alarmed when she realised the gravity of the situation and the identity of her predator. A horrifying scream of fear threatened to let loose from her throat when she saw his face.

But the predator had his grip nice and strong, making it very tough to dislodge. She caved in under his relentless pressure. Feeling the struggle lessen, he managed to forcefully undress her saree and with enough force, ripped the undergarment off, lost along with her integrity. Struggling like a prey that she was seen as; he clamped her mouth shut with his left hand like pliers.

He, the predator, very well knew his next chain of action, thrusting himself forcefully as he raped her soul, and at the same time, to appease his musing, he harshly whispered into her ear, "You said I could not do it, right? What have you to say now, you slut? Go and let your lover know how you were enjoying in my arms; I bet you will not tell him as he may dump you. Say you are enjoying it now, why don't you? Eh?"

Finished, he got up, glancing at the now broken figure of Ira in tatters and slouched away as a smile of satisfaction and supremacy dawned on his face, not knowing that the moral strings within his mind had snapped as he had dominated and overwhelmed a helpless girl. In ignorance and in bliss, he did not realise that this satisfaction stemmed from a much greater evil draped over cowardice. As he took his first step towards becoming a 'predator', he lost his humanity and at the same time, the qualification to be remembered as a man, the sole intent behind this disgraceful and evil act.

Rape leaves behind an unforgettable scar; tainting the soul of the victim, something that would haunt Ira throughout her life in this world. It remained to be seen how Ira would cope with this attack on her, but for sure, she would for a long time be unable to soar to her potential, as the world would point fingers at her, seemingly gazing directly at that mark etched on her soul, forever.

The neurons in her brain would be crushed by the repeated memoirs of this assault.

Returning back, Bhiku was in a different zone now. He was sure that she would not leave her work as she was left with no other options. It was only a question of time before he caught them at the shacks. On his recce before, he had noticed that the doors of the shacks were flimsy; designed only for privacy and not to keep an intruder out.

Some three Saturdays later, he saw the auto parked outside a shack, grabbed his hammer, and rushed with revenge in his mind. He hit the door with his shoulder, breaking it in one go and landed inside.

There they were, naked and entwined in throes of passion. By the time realisation dawned on them, it was too late. Viki, on top, got two thwacks on his head and his body just slithered down the bed. A cacophony could be heard outside as the watchman came rushing with his stick. Bhiku only had a single chance to hit Ira, as he landed one blow on her right cheek.

Other passers-by stopped, and soon, there was commotion. Some people rushed in to rescue Ira. In the meantime, Bhiku ran out of the shack and rushed to his shanty. Closing it from inside, he breathed hard, thinking about what he had done and contemplated on the outcome. He did not realise that he could very well be labelled as the person behind this incident, either by Ira or by the person who glanced at his face.

Soon, the police arrived and began an investigation, but first, Viki was rushed to a close-by nursing home in a comatose state. Ira had a broken cheek bone and few broken teeth, but she still managed to identify Bhiku as the culprit of her assault. Later the same morning, he was picked up and on the statement of Ira, an FIR was lodged.

In the police lock-up, he was thrashed around by the constables, who were keen on finding the reason behind him committing these crimes. The charge sheet included rape and assault, along with second-degree attempt to murder. There were witnesses and, in any case, he had already confessed. It was two months before the case came up in front of a Judge in the sessions court.

Enough interest was piled up on this case amongst the people, and many had crowded the court room where Justice Iqbal was presiding.

The court had already appointed a lawyer to defend Bhiku and it was soon made clear to the court that Bhiku was a 17-year-old juvenile, and therefore could not be tried in the court. Observing the evidence provided, the learned Judge agreed and ordered that Bhiku was to be sent to the government juvenile detention centre and was to be released after turning the age of 18.

Bhiku was really lucky that age was on his side, and that

for a very serious crime, his punishment was basically nothing. He would be busy in the centre and would be released within one year. No big deal for him.

The punishment hardly justified the gory crimes he had committed, but that was the way law worked. Unlike the clutches of evil beyond the domain of law, everything was bound with restrictions; even the law itself. There would be no repentance and Bhiku would proceed to feel all-powerful with his ventures. In his mind, he had already justified what he had done.

ARRIVING AT RINKUNAGAR

Life was quite cushy at the juvenile detention centre, as Bhiku adapted to it nice and fine. All inmates were handed tasks to complete, and they were not allowed to step outside the facility which was guarded by police night and day. He was deputed to work in the carpentry shed, which was totally fine by him.

But humans were social creatures, and so, many of the inmates had formed mini gangs in the centre, which they used to flex their muscles now and then. Disagreement on any issue could lead to viscous fistfights. The gangs wanted him to join them, but Bhiku was not interested, as he did not want to land himself in any trouble. But the unending taunts branded him as a coward. He snorted when he heard it; he could be accused of any misdemeanour but not cowardice, for that would be pointing fingers at his 'manliness'.

The one particular gang that finally got under his goatee was a gang led by a tall, gangling teenager named Arif, who used to pick up fights for no rhyme or reason, just wanting to lord over the inmates. Bhiku was aware of his reputation but was not bothered, as he had some degree of confidence in his physical abilities.

Arif, escorted by two gang members, waylaid Bhiku near the common toilets. The very fact that two members were with Arif proved that he was not as confident as he looked, and this pleased Bhiku's ego. He was at ease and well aware that Arif would be the one to make the first move.

"Why are you such a coward? You keep yourself aloof; are you hiding something? What crime did you commit? I am giving you one last chance to join my gang." Bhiku kept quiet, just watching every movement and gesture of Arif in a cool and calm manner with eyes filled with disdain. That was until Arif pushed him, demanding an answer.

"Don't touch me," the predator from within him growled as he continued, "I am not interested in joining any gang. Just get out of my way," he said in a quiet and overbearing voice.

His parole officer had informed him that he had about a year left in this detention centre. But with good behaviour, he could land a 3-month early release. The parole board met every month, and he did not want to jeopardise his chances; that was the reason behind him keeping a low profile.

Arif again taunted him, uttering the word coward again. This time, he arrived close to Bhiku, glaring at him right in the eye, unleashing a challenge. Sensing that Arif would try to hit him in the stomach, Bhiku took a fast step backwards, pivoted on his left heel using it as a fulcrum, and balancing his body, slammed his right leg right on the testicles of Arif who crumpled and howled with grief and pain.

The other two boys were stunned seeing what had happened. They turned and fled. The soul-wrenching howls of Arif attracted the guards, who came running in and caught hold of Bhiku, dragging him to the warden's office. The warden heard out Bhiku's reasoning and dismissed him, but not before warning him that one more incidence of violence would mean cancelling of the parole he was to be offered.

There was an uneasy truce within the apprehensive environment for about a month, before Arif, thirsty for revenge, caught him unaware in the dimly lit corridor located in front of the library. Bhiku had just come out after reading a newspaper where an article had appeared, stating how bad these detention centres were run, and how deep they were mired in corruption, both physical and financial.

When he turned around the corner to the staircase, Arif jumped on him, hitting him on his head with a small stone, and for a moment, Bhiku blacked out. But he did not lose control and realised he was in deep danger. He got hold of himself in one swift movement and grabbed Arif's collar, dragging him towards the railing, found good balance and slammed Arif's head on the steel railing. Arif lost his footing and slipped, falling down the staircase, slamming his head on every step. He managed to scream and invited attention of the police guards, who rushed to apprehend Bhiku. By the time Arif went spiralling down the stairs, he had lost consciousness, but clearly, that looked like trouble.

While Bhiku was detained, Arif was rushed to a hospital

where they found that he had fractured an arm and his right ankle apart from having a serious head injury when Bhiku had slammed his head on the railing.

In absence of any eyewitness to support Bhiku stating that he had been attacked; an FIR was filed for attempted murder. But just as before, he was let off being a juvenile, and his chances of parole were dismissed. The Judge was now of the opinion that Bhiku had proved himself to be really dangerous in the juvenile detention and other minors' well-being couldn't be risked. "I feel that the culprit should be shifted to central jail but will be placed under police protection, not allowed to mingle with other jailed inmates. He will be released on his 18th birthday. So ordered."

Bhiku had three more months to live in incarceration before his release and the start of a new life. He hoped he would not be targeted in central jail; he had heard some dramatic stories that leaked out from the jail of how the old inmates preyed on newcomers.

He had to be really careful.

The very first morning, while waiting to eat his breakfast, he was accosted by two vicious-looking characters. They gave him a lecherous smile and made gestures filled with sexual overtones. First, he avoided them, but then, they pushed him into a corner and whispered, "Lalaram is our guru, he has asked you to meet him tonight after dinner. Just make sure you are there, or you will regret landing in this jail."

Bhiku was stunned by this vile and transparent threat. He reported this to his supposed police guards, but they merely shrugged their shoulders and informed him that they would not interfere in any matter. They would only intervene if someone attacked him physically.

"Anyway, Lalaram is the real power in this jail. You will be protected under his shade, and no one would dare to approach you." Clearly, these guards were on his payroll.

After dinner, he found three criminals following him as he walked fast to his cell, only to see the police guards. Being outnumbered, he realised that he had no option but to accompany them to Lalaram.

Lalaram had a well-built physique, his whole body emanating a menacing aura with a deep scar that trailed from his cheekbone and reached the right earlobe, a clear indication of a knife attack. With a low husky voice, he welcomed Bhiku and took him inside the cell. "Don't worry, no harm will come to you as you will be known as my intimate friend. I know you are here only for three months, so have a good stay." There were 6 inmates in the cell, and they made an exit only to stand guard outside.

Lalaram ordered Bhiku to disrobe and then had his way with the terrified boy. Bhiku cried in pain as Lalaram went on to rape him, using his body to satisfy his lust. A helpless Bhiku was then escorted to his cell, but not before he was told to present himself again tomorrow at same time. He was ordered to perform orally on Lalaram. This became the ritual and a terrorised Bhiku could not turn to anyone for help. Eventually, in about a month, Lalaram became tired of Bhiku, and the target of his lust was directed to other recent newcomers that were admitted to the central jail. But Bhiku slowly recovered physically; mentally, he was still a wreck. Lalaram's dictate was still helpful as no one forced themselves on Bhiku.

Just a month was left when the head warden of the female jail adjacent to central jail sent for him. Again, he had no choice but to do her bidding. A really muscular and tough-looking woman, she had no time for inane talks and simply demanded her needs. With the escort party standing guard, Bhiku had nowhere to run. He just caved in, thinking only about the date when he would be free, doing what he was ordered. A thoroughly humiliated and broken Bhiku returned to his cell. The police guards just smirked and laughed at his now broken soul and deflated ego. It was here that the darkest of the evils lurked.

Used and abused, he was finally released, but he was by now a sort of hardened criminal and wanted to seek revenge from the world at large.

He was not sure where to go, but somehow reached Rinkunagar. He liked what he saw. But he also knew he had to create a gang of his own if he was to induce terror in the world. At the corner tea stall, he asked some questions and came to know the identity of the man who was crowned as the big 'gunda' locally. He was Chandu, who was used to extorting money from local shopkeepers after a promise of protection. Bhiku knew what he had to do and silently went about this task.

TERROR ESTABLISHED

It would be difficult to form his own gang at a rapid speed, so he decided to seize an already established one. A straight-in-the-face answer was humiliating Chandu in front of his henchmen and few of the shops. Word travelled fast in the neighbourhood and shopkeepers would pay obeisance to the newly crowned King of the criminal world.

He tailed Chandu for a couple of days. He realised that his plan would enable him to hit two birds with one stone. Firstly, Chandu's gang would either disperse or would kneel in obedience of their new master, so he would inherit followers who would know the ins and outs of the slum. Secondly, extortion money would start coming to him, so financially, he would stabilise.

Chandu used to go for morning rounds, collecting protection money and to flex his muscles on any shopkeeper running behind on the payment. So, he decided to run into him and insult him at his *'adda'* or corner where most shops were established.

So, that morning, the moment he saw Chandu and his four guards, he walked towards the group on purpose and deliberately pushed Chandu's right shoulder; before the surprised man could react, Bhiku snarled loudly, "Oye! Are you blind or something? You can't see that you almost rammed into me? Next time this happens, I will break your arm." He then dusted himself.

Chandu, pressing the shoulder where Bhiku had pushed him hard, emerged from his surprised trance and caught hold of Bhiku's T-shirt, pulling him right in front. He cocked his hand and fist, as if wanting to hit him square on the face.

"You motherfucker! Either you apologise now, or I will split your face open. You will know what it means to take '*panga*' (mess) with me." He was really angry.

Bhiku taunted him more, at the same time being mentally and physically alert, awaiting the first move from Chandu. "*Chal, chal,* get lost. I am not afraid of a bully like you. If your goons were not with you, I would have taught you a lesson in civil behaviour."

Now, Chandu was really riled up as he gestured to his men, indicating not to interfere. "Bastard! I do not need any help to smother insects like you."

Trying to hit Bhiku on his face, he did not expect such a fast reaction from the boy and his fist simply hit air, making his body tumble after losing his balance. Bhiku turned on the balls of his feet as he caught hold of the hand by grabbing his wrist and twisted it inward, shattering the wrist. He did not stop, and kept on pressing hard even as Chandu howled, screaming in pain on top of his voice.

The pressure was unrelenting, and Bhiku was merciless as he pushed Chandu down and told him, "Kiss my shoes if you want me to leave you and promise not to come here again, ever."

"Yes, yes, I will go and will not come here again," Chandu yelled, kissing the floor, and crawled towards Bhiku's shoes and kissing them as he was asked. One could see the bone splinters in that wrist. Chandu limped away as he held his broken wrist with his other hand. The whole charade took about 40 seconds.

The gang members were too mortified to speak, and so were the shopkeepers around. They slowly approached him and thanked him for getting rid of that goon, Chandu. "I am new here; I am taking over and will protect your business. It will cost more, but there will be no incidents as long as you people co-operate. And what about you two from Chandu's gang? Will you join me now, or you also want to leave from here?"

The two guys fell at his feet and swore allegiance, total loyalty. That was it, simple and fast. He had now become the new face that would terrorise the slum. He had just established himself and was satisfied with this situation. The two gang members, the first ones of the Bhiku gang, took him to their hideout place where six others were waiting.

The situation was explained to them, and they immediately agreed to join Bhiku. Word spread fast that Chandu was out, and new power had emerged in the name of Bhiku. He ordered the gang to arrange a meet with each and every shopkeeper, asking the protection money they were paying, which would be increased by 15 percent, and that they were to bring it with them. He wanted the residents and the shopkeepers to fear him, and so, he had to kill the chicken to warn the monkeys.

His gang handed him the intel about a couple of shopkeepers who had always denied Chandu the *hafta* as they said that they knew some police constables from the police station. They felt that there was no need to cough up the protection money.

"Here, I am the police, I am the King. They shall pay as I desire; otherwise, I will shut your shop down. I will not ask you again. I want to see the money tomorrow. Now get out."

Other shopkeepers drifted in with the money and Bhiku soon collected a good amount. They all said that the money would be handed over to the collection agents deputed by Bhiku. That evening, he went to the local police station to meet and greet the Senior Inspector in charge. It was Kamble, and he looked up from the file he was reading, indicating Bhiku to sit down.

"Yes," he grunted, and asked, "what can I do for you? Have you come to file a report or something?"

Bhiku, who was carrying a big fat envelope, just pushed it across as he waited for Kamble to see what was inside. Tearing it open, his eyes were glued to the contents, but at the same time, he opened one of his drawers and slid the envelope inside with a seasoned flourish. His eyes sparkling, whispering in a low voice he again asked, "What is this for? We have not even met before."

Bhiku explained that this was a token for the inspector.

"There will be more, as I have just taken over the duty of protecting people in Rinkunagar. You shall receive our goodwill gesture monthly and on time for all the hard work that you have done for the people. But you know, there might be some people who would want to create chaos. I just want *Sahib* to go easy on reports against me. I will ensure you are compensated for your efforts."

Kamble was impressed and shook his hands as he had a lecherous smile on his face.

"I assure you, there will be nothing from my side that will hamper your duty of protecting the people. I like your style; it will be nice working with you." Bhiku smiled and left in good spirits.

With the police backing him, he now wanted support from the local political power, and he knew what was to be done. From the time he had met Kamble, Bhiku understood that the inspector was totally going to be loyal to Bhiku. The police inspector had watery eyes with veins on his face standing out, the true mark of an alcoholic. He also had a twitch on his right wrist which kept shivering at times. Bhiku also realised after a couple of meetings that Kamble was also a pervert and a lustful man who was always willing to taste the flesh of any female that Bhiku was able to arrange. So, as long as the cash and women kept on flowing, Kamble would overlook the crimes committed by Bhiku, landing him complete control of Rinkunagar.

Indeed, this was exactly what was happening in the slum. Most of the inhabitants were illiterate and did not understand the ways of the world. The brutalised and raped women did want to register an FIR or a written complaint against Bhiku, but Kamble had instructed his staff at the police station that victims of Bhiku who wanted to file complaints be sent to him.

He would patiently hear them and write down the complaint of the hapless victims but never wrote what they actually said. He also ensured that there would be many loopholes left in the FIR which Bhiku would use to escape time and again.

Sometimes, if the victim looked nice and young, he would make the woman wait in the waiting room and then call for Bhiku. Kamble being a senior inspector had his own chamber, a small room with a bathroom right behind his desk. The chamber was used for resting and refreshing himself when he was on 24 hours duty and to conduct secret meetings. The room had a backdoor, so that if he wanted then, he could come in and go out without being noticed by anyone in his cabin.

It was in this cabin that Bhiku entered and waited for Kamble to bring in the victim who was daring enough to file a complaint. The entire police station knew what went inside the chamber but didn't dare to interfere. They, in fact, kept guard outside. The staff was also bribed enough by Bhiku now and then to ensure that he actually had total control over the station. Thus, the victim was brutalised again without fear, by both Bhiku and Kamble.

The inspector actually came from a police background as his father was also a policeman. His father had unfortunately passed away during communal riots when Avinash was just finishing his graduation.

As a rule, one member of the martyred policeman's family was given a job under the sympathy factor. Avinash

Kamble, which was his full name, joined the force immediately after his graduation exams, as an ASI or Assistant Sub-Inspector. Two years of training made him physically strong and mentally equipped to take on the job in earnest. And with stars in his eyes, a feeling of sincere nationalism, he started his career off. He knew how corruption had seeped in the police forces and swore to himself that he would not fall prey to the scourge of corruption.

His late father used to lament the fact that the society always blamed the police for anything wrong and never appreciated when the police performed their task with aplomb.

Whenever they got a raise in salary, eyebrows were raised by everyone, including the politicians whom they served day-in and day-out. Everyone cursed them, insisting that the police were just not doing their task. They were abused if they did not do their job properly and cursed if they overreacted in a situation and a 'gunda' got hurt or shot in public disturbances.

His father often said that this was a thankless job. The salaries were much below what was paid in the private sector and duty hours were obnoxious.

Frequently, he was on a job of 48 hours nonstop when there was VIP movement or if there was hint of social unrest, and then was called back on duty with just 4-5 hours of uneasy sleep. No wonder most of the force was suffering from BP, hypertension, obesity, and other ailments like sleeping disorders.

They also started drinking alcohol, slowly at first, and

then in abundance, as after imbibing alcohol, they could defeat insomnia for some time and sleep well enough to sustain the working day the next morning.

This alcoholism also brought in problems in the house, especially with wives, neglected families, and liver diseases. And of course, bribing and corruption soon followed, as now, to sustain the expenses in the house, his drinking, and other habits, he needed more and more money.

It started with small gifts and small envelopes, but soon, he became greedy enough to demand outright cash which was to be sent to his house. He had got married when he turned 25 and had two children.

His wife had become used to living it up as there was abundance of cash and luxury items flowing in from the money obtained from the bribe. Sometimes, when cash was too much to keep in house or the bank locker, he asked for jewellery. The wife never complained, and as he got promoted to Sub-Inspector and then to Inspector and now as Senior Inspector, the bribery and gifts had now become more lavish.

But Kamble knew the police system and greased it accordingly by keeping his seniors happy. True, there were many honest and straight police personnel, and he ensured that he remained outside the radar of such officials.

And when, as Sub-Inspector and Inspector, some bars and ladies' bars came under his jurisdiction, he was slowly persuaded to sleep with any of the girls he found interesting. His wife had come to know about it, but she turned a blind eye as she was just happy wallowing in luxury and abundance of cash. "Why rock the boat?" She would say to herself. Thus, Avinash Kamble was simply the best person Bhiku could think of as the policeman in charge of his area.

THE BADSHAH OF RINKUNAGAR

The two shopkeepers did not come the next day as they were ordered. Bhiku sent his gang members to get them here with the money in two days' time, giving them a chance to come clean and accept his domination. Yet, they informed his members they would not come.

Hearing this, he saw red and decided to teach them a lesson. The first target was a shop dealing with jeans and T-shirts. The owner, Sanjeev, was sitting at the counter. Bhiku raced in and caught hold of the man and hauled him outside as he started raining blows right, left, and centre. The gang members were not allowed to interfere as they kept guard to ensure that no one else came too close. Sanjeev was trying to fight back in some manner, but he had no chance against this rugged, strong man who found great pleasure in fistfights. After satisfying his anger with sheer and naked violence, important not only for his ego but also to set an example to others, he showed what he was capable of when really angry.

It was only when Sanjeev was in a semi-conscious state

that Bhiku stopped and ordered his gang to get some water, splashing him on Sanjeev's face to make him alert. Bhiku snarled, *"Haramzade, tere ko bola tha mere se panga nahi lena par tu mana nahi.* (I had told you not to mess with me but you didn't listen.) Now, you will pay the price of refusing my orders. *Chal*, get the money or I will break your hand to start with." There was total silence from the local residents who had gathered to observe what was happening.

Sanjeev mumbled something to Bhiku who did not like what the man was saying and roared that he wanted money now.

"Tere ghar pe hoga paisa. Chal, abhi chal. (You'll have money at home. Take me there.)"

He told his gang to haul the man up and drag him to his house. There was a commotion as they neared the house. Sanjeev's wife came running out and embraced the man with a bloodied cheek and marks of fight all over his body because of the thrashing he had received.

"Please leave him alone, I beg you; show some mercy. What has he done?" she enquired sobbing, not knowing why her husband was singled out.

By this time, Bhiku and his entourage, still dragging Sanjeev, had entered the house. Sanjeev approached a nearby cabinet and from a thick wad of currency notes, counting what was demanded of him and handed the same to Bhiku. "This amount was for yesterday. Today, you have made me very angry, and as a penalty you shall give me the rest that you are holding." Snatching away the balance from Sanjeev's hand, Bhiku marched outside but not before yelling at Sanjeev that he should not go to police, "Or I will come again."

The other shopkeeper received the message and had closed his shop with the money waiting at the hideout. The moment he saw Bhiku, he rushed and fell at his feet, blabbering that he had made a mistake and pleaded for forgiveness.

"Okay but bring extra 10 percent as penalty for not listening to me. In one hour, I want that cash, now go," said the new King of Crime.

The man brought the balance within the hour. Now, with enough cash in his hands, he took out a good amount and placed the notes in an envelope, which he sealed.

The evening saw him going to the residence of MLA Rana Patil and seeking an audience. He was ushered in, and he told Rana's secretary that he had a gift for the boss. He was taken to Rana's personal chamber behind the office and asked to wait.

In a few minutes, the boss sauntered in and came to the point immediately. "I have a meeting in ten minutes. So, hurry up with the business," and lit a cigarette.

Bhiku took out the envelope and handed it to Rana, whose grim expression turned into a soft smile. He raised his eyebrows enquiringly. "Sir, I am from Rinkunagar and have brought a small token for you. This will be done every month. I will also work for you. I request you to kindly overlook any complaints you may get about my method of working."

Rana was silent as he took a few puffs. Then he

enquired, "You are the fellow who threw Chandu out. I never liked him anyway, the good-for-nothing fellow. Look; just don't go overboard, try not to be too messy. I can protect you to some extent but not for serious crimes. Otherwise, I will be happy to keep you in my sight."

This was what Bhiku wanted. He touched Rana's feet and sauntered back to Rinkunagar. He now had both police and the required political protection along with the liberty to do what he wanted.

Soon, his connections were tested when within a fortnight, Sanjeev's wife went to file a complaint against him at the police station. Kamble sent a constable to brief him. Bhiku reached the police station just in time to see the woman hurrying away.

"I told her that since there were no women constables present, we shall file no complaint. Now tell me what you want done?" asked Kamble.

"Just make an FIR that fails before the magistrate. Rest, I will see what needs to be done." He rushed out, thanking Kamble.

Reaching Rinkunagar, he got hold of his 6 gang members and rushed to Sanjeev's shanty. Breaking open the door, he barged in. While two gang members got hold of Sanjeev, he caught hold of the wife and tore open her clothes, slapped her a couple of times and proceeded to molest her in front of the helpless husband. Satisfied, he got up and threatened, "This is just a trailer. If you go for an FIR tomorrow, I will strip you naked in public." Leaving behind the words, he went away. A stunned Sanjeev could only watch in horror as this happened.

Bhiku got bolder and bolder as time passed by, and like a predator, he stalked his victims and barged into their homes, or just picked them up and brought them to his hideout.

He caught hold of Deepa one night as she walked home and raped her under a bush close to her shanty. He could make out who was timid and who was a little volatile. One day, he waylaid two sisters whom he had already abused before, put them in an autorickshaw and took them to the police station, whispering something in Kamble's ears.

A smiling Kamble and Bhiku boarded the police jeep, forcing the sisters inside and took them to an isolated place. Kamble then, after satisfying his lust, had become a partner in crime. Bhiku would obtain more freedom. Now, with the inspector having turned his attention away from Bhiku, the rapist could do whatever he wanted. Kamble was there to protect him.

There were strong rumours that he had murdered three men, including the shopkeeper Sanjeev whose body was later found at a railway crossing nearby. Two other men who had rubbed Bhiku the wrong way but were residents of Rinkunagar, had disappeared in mysterious circumstances.

No one dared to oppose the man who was now the personification of evil, with no remorse for his actions. He had established his terror as he desired.

I KILLED BHIKU

Present

Asha Patil returned from the court and found that things had gone as she and other women had planned. The fateful decision taken not so long ago was simple. As soon as the next FIR had been lodged against Bhiku, the women had kept a sharp eye on his arrival for bail hearing. There were two who waited outside the central jail gate on that fateful day. As soon as he came out with the police escort, the women rushed back to the slum with the news.

Asha did not go to the court, but she choreographed every move. Deepa was in charge at the court along with fifty other women.

As decided, they all were armed with a kitchen knife, pepper and the spiced concoction. They stood outside the court gate, waiting for Bhiku to arrive from the police vehicle. Another group of women waited further away. They were to join when he was being attacked in order to totally confuse the police and the court security staff. They were thoroughly disappointed when the hearing had been postponed, but they suppressed their feelings about the last day of their torture. After all, it was going to be worth it.

The next day, as soon as the vehicle came in sight, the women became alert. Deepa was now inside the station premises, and once she saw Bhiku, she signalled the waiting gang, and they came rushing in.

The group led by Deepa came rushing in and attacked him with full force. Indeed, the planning was super.

As soon as he was viciously stabbed and '*Mukti*' slogans started to reverberate around the court, Deepa and the group left hurriedly, and another group took their place. Bhiku was butchered many times. The women ensured that he died a horrific death.

This group rushed back to Rinkunagar, where Asha was waiting to start the next part of the plan.

The women disappeared in their shanties by the time Gulabrao arrived. With no one listening to him and Asha being released by Justice Inamdar, there was no option left, except for forcing a few of the perpetrators. He had the police loudspeaker and addressed the slum by standing in their main meeting area. "I have to arrest some of you. You can't hide and run away. It's better you surrender peacefully. I have got female constables with me, and they have orders to be tough with you lot. So, I shall count to ten and then proceed to arrest the first ten women, dragging them out from inside their houses." He started counting slowly, but even at the count 8 not a single soul emerged.

He was hesitant to count to 10 but had to count anyway.

As if on a signal, at the count of 10, all shanties opened

and out stepped a woman with a placard: "I killed Bhiku, arrest me."

The police party was stunned deeply. They had no idea about how to proceed. Gulabrao was rendered speechless and just couldn't react. The first few women slowly occupied the jeep, while the rest started a brisk walk to the court.

It was a sight to see so many claiming credit for assassinating the dreaded criminal. At the court premises, they started chanting, "I killed Bhiku, arrest me." The court had been closed for the day, so they decided to sleep in the premises and catch Judge Inamdar as soon as he would arrive.

Kamble and his team could not do anything. After all, one could perhaps catch someone who had committed 200 rapes and murders, but on what basis would one arrest over 200 people for one murder? In a catch, both sides kept their wary eyes on each other. Kamble knew he would be in for a hauling once the Judge entered the premises. The Judge would make him walk on burning coal.

At sharp 9:30 a.m., Inamdar's car entered the premises and came to a thudding halt. The driver told him that he had no place to park, as everywhere, women with placards were lying down. At a signal from Deepa, the women got up and started chanting, "I killed Bhiku, arrest me."

Justice Inamdar looked happy and at peace, as the car issue was resolved with Sheila, at least for the time being and the two had after a long time, had their amorous moments that night. He immediately understood what was happening and walked away to his chambers with a smile, while the women went to his courtroom. They packed the court room; more were outside at the door.

Inamdar sent for Kamble immediately and loudly questioned him, "Why don't you arrest all of them? After all, they are claiming they killed your partner in crime."

"No, Sir," Kamble interjected, "I had nothing to do with him."

The Judge persisted, "Then why was he never arrested? Rinkunagar was under your jurisdiction, yet you never took a step. You had to be conniving with him. The petition of the woman who complained said this fellow was involved in hundreds of rape cases and the helpless victims went to file FIR many times, but you and other staff never co-operated. What is that supposed to mean?"

He ordered that the women confessing to the crime be arrested immediately. "But Sir, there are some 250 to 300 women out there. In which lockup should I take them? The lockup in my station can only accommodate 10 women at the maximum capacity."

"That is your problem," the Judge said but asked the leader of these women to step forward so that he could understand what really was going on.

Kamble stayed put as Inamdar had not dismissed him. Deepa stepped forward, and on being questioned, she gave him the entire story of Bhiku and what had transpired in Rinkunagar. She told him about the way he had terrorised the *'basti'* in a more crueller manner.

"Sir," she said, "I will give you just a few examples of what the evil named Bhiku was. He dragged a woman out of her house, cut her ears off to get the gold earrings and then let two of his henchmen rape her. He would wake up victims in their houses at around 4:00-5:00 a.m., when they would be sleepy. Pretending to be a policeman, he would wait for the door to be opened, and if it did, he would drag the victim out and rape her. Once, he stripped a man naked, burnt him with cigarette butts, and forced him to dance in front of his 16-year-old daughter, proceeding to rape her in front of her sobbing father."

Deepa told the Judge that she herself was raped on three such occasions. She openly told the Judge, "I am sorry to tell you that you have failed the society and people like you are as much to blame as you never took a serious note of what Bhiku was up to. The sweet-talking MLA, who came begging for our votes, failed us as he was just a normal politician who, like others of his ilk, betrayed the democratic process, and our so-called *Lok Tantra*'. So, I just want to say here that women of Rinkunagar have not committed a crime. We just took the law in our hands because the responsible ones wouldn't and rendered justice to the evil that tormented our lives."

The Judge listened to Deepa with rapt attention and smiled slightly when she told Judge that Kamble was hands-n-glove with Bhiku. The Judge was just waiting to hear this.

"Luckily, this case will now be under the Home Ministry. They shall decide the next course. But you know that I admire you and your friends. You all displayed great courage. But as the law states, one cannot take it into their own hands, unless there was question of self-defence. That itself is a very thin line. I am glad I don't have to hand out the judgement. But off the record, I can agree with you and say that if Rinkunagar victims of such a dreaded and evil man were pushed to take law in their own hands, it was because the law and law-enforcing agencies had failed in their duty by not giving them succour."

Before going back to chambers, he on his own motion ordered three months jail for Kamble and six months' suspension without salary. The Senior Inspector was stunned as he heard what the Judge said, but not even a squeak emerged from his mouth.

"Do you know what it means? If I had come to know and there was any evidence that stated your involvement in terrifying the victims along with the deceased, I would have had you arrested immediately. You are lucky that I did not have you jailed for years." He ordered the Court Marshall to do the needful with Avinash Kamble and waited till the inspector was handcuffed, before leaving for his chambers.

The women trooped back to the slum where Asha waited to hear what had happened at the court. Deepa hugged her and relayed her the entire story. She was overwhelmed as tears cascaded from her eyes. The never-ending ordeal was finally over. Now, the women of Rinkunagar could breathe easy and walk without fear.

Deepa asked her, "How did you know none of us would be caught and arrested?"

"There exists a time when the need arises for us to take law in our hands and defend ourselves. I knew if we stayed united, nothing would happen. Togetherness is power. And there is so much public opinion against Bhiku that it would be very, very difficult for any government authority to side with him. I factored all this in. Anyways, what is done is done. Let us forget this nightmare and carry on with our lives. We have attained '*Mukti*' at last."

ACKNOWLEDGEMENTS

Again, as in my last book, Match Point, I happily acknowledge the work of the young team from my publisher, Inkfeathers: Uma, Sagar, Ritwik, Kashish. Right from the time I narrated the outline of Mukti to Sagar, he told me he got goosebumps.

Ritwik said that this book is one of a kind and every woman should read it.

For Uma, Mukti is like self-realisation. The book should give courage to the women after reading. What the characters suffer from and get, they come back to seek revenge.

INKFEATHERS PUBLISHING

India's Most Author Friendly Publishing House

Stay updated about the latest books, anthologies, events, exclusive offers, contests, product giveaways and other things that we do to support authors.

f   Inkfeathers Publishing

O   @InkfeathersPublishing

y   @_Inkfeathers

in   @Inkfeathers

⊕   Inkfeathers.com

We'd love to connect with you!